Tears of Queens

Tanzy Alexis

TANZY ALEXIS

ISBN: 0985418717
ISBN: 978-098541871

DEDICATION

I dedicate this book to every queen of every hue, young and old, single and married. God created you on purpose! You should already know that you are fearfully and wonderfully made, but I pray God expresses this to you more vividly in this book.

ACKNOWLEDGMENTS

I have to most definitely give a heartfelt thanks to God for trusting me with this book and for protecting my gift to write. I thank you for this journey, though very tough at times and unbearably painful; God we did it again, together!

To my Mom and Dad, Joann and Stanley Island: I love you so very much for everything, including sticking with me when I lost everything. I thank you for your continued support as I make strides to get it all back and then some. To my sister and brother: I love you both dearly and pray God's best for your life.

To my sister queen, Ashley and your husband Deundre Grice: you both inspire me in so many ways! I believe true love exists because of you two. Can't wait for God to bless y'all with weetots, so I can love on them!

To my sister queen, Ashlee "Ashalina" Lewis: I never knew a woman like you existed. You're the sweetest thing I've ever known (In my Lauryn Hill voice). I love you and your cute little family. Thank you for accepting my proposition. I'm eagerly anticipating a surprise that will screw up your impeccable vocabulary.

To the three musketeers, Tatianah Green, Alicia Spikes, and Genevieve, I mean Geneise Grant: you ladies rock and I love you to pieces! Thanks for all of your help and support over the course of the time I've known you all.

To Pastor Jedidiah Brown of Chosen Generation Church, thank you for showing me another side of ministry, love you to life! Janice Miller, you're the best! Kenneth Griffin, you already know what it is! All we do is WIN! Christina Edwards, my angel, I love you too with my whole heart! And to anyone I've missed, whom I've met during various times of my life: I blow you all kisses! Don't forget G.I.N.O...GOD IS NUMBER ONE!

TEARS OF QUEENS

Prologue

Ari's current situation: Noah had just told her to stay put outside his townhome, but her basic instincts were pushing her to make a move. After having found her beautiful art gallery vandalized and practically destroyed earlier, Ari was a little out of it. She glanced over at a butterfly bush to see a spray paint can without its lid. She kicked over the can to read the label, *"Krylon, Gloss, Cherry Red"*. Ari reached in her purse to retrieve her cell phone and quickly dialed 911.

"911 operator speaking, what is your emergency?' The female operator asked.

"Someone is about to die," Ari was able to spew through clenched teeth.

She gave the operator the address to the place where she was prepared to kill someone out of nothing but pure rage. Ari walked into the home and straight up the stairs. She heard Noah asking someone to pray with him, and her face turned up with confusion.

POW!

Ari's eyes bulged when she heard the sound of a single gunshot coming from inside of the room where she had just heard Noah's voice. That sound pierced her ears and rippled through her body. Fear lost the battle to her anger and curiosity as she ran into the room to see a woman in a grey jogging suit standing over Noah with a gun. Without any further hesitation, she lunged toward the woman to tackle her. The woman flailed violently and the gun flew out of her hands.

The two women fought frantically and ferociously. The fight led into the hallway as Ari continued to give this woman, who had more upper body strength than she, her entire might.

The woman managed to grab a hold of a full chunk of Ari's curly mane and Ari screamed in agony. At that point, Ari thought she could no longer make fun of all the girls she'd seen in the past, who found themselves caught in one of these grips. Typically, she had concluded that the hair is what all girls went for first, so why wasn't she ready for this?

They fell onto the landing at the top of the stairs, which gave the woman in the grey jogging suit a slight advantage, since she was now on top of Ari choking her. This wasn't the first time Ari had been choked. Her own mother had once strangled her until she blacked out. Ari's strength waned until the woman's face seemed to morph into her mother's. She didn't die then, and she wasn't going to die now! Ari reached up to the woman's face and attempted to gouge her eyes out. The woman screamed, and Ari removed her from atop her body. She then quickly crawled over to the woman and pummeled her senseless.

"Stay where you are! Put your hands where we can see them and stay where you are," A male police officer shouted with his gun pointed at her.

Ari obeyed. A stupefied cloud surrounded her, as another officer came up the stairs and placed handcuffs around her wrists. The officer led Ari down the stairs. She was intoxicated by a mixture of poisonous thoughts which caused her to go into a daze. This moment, this very moment, seemed like nothing but a terrible dream. Her daze was broken when she thought of Noah.

"She shot him! He's upstairs! She shot him!" Ari screamed.

The officer placed Ari in the back of the squad car and closed the door. Ari saw the woman in the grey jogging suit staggering from inside the home. The woman then quickly ran away.

"Hey! Hey! There she is! Go stop her," Ari yelled frantically.

She sat in silence after that. There was nothing else she could do in the back of a squad car. Unfortunately, this wasn't the first time she sat in the back of one of these vehicles either.

PART 1

QUEEN ARI
"She needs help with lady stuff."

August 2000

Ari looked at the tissue and saw blood, "Oh my God!"

She had officially started her period today- something she'd been dreading since her first lesson on menstrual cycles in a Sex Ed class two years ago. Apprehension served as a shield against the jokes a few girls threw for not coming on her cycle yet. Ari figured the delay must have been due to sexual inactivity, since her hecklers were promiscuous. Well, that tissue in her hands proved her wrong. Immediately after Ari wiped herself a second time, terrible pains shot through her abdomen. She hunched over in agony. When the pain seemed to have subsided for a while, she sat back up, folded a hand full of tissue into a makeshift panty-liner, and placed it into her panties before she flushed the toilet.

She washed her face and wiped it with a face towel. Once completely dry, she stared at the reflection of the girl who was looking back at her. She should have known this was coming. Her face had warned her of her menstrual arrival with its sudden hideous breakout. The breakout was gone, but the scars remained. Ari no longer felt like the innocent and pure girl she was a few days prior. She felt flawed and ugly. As she wiped shame that crept from her eyes, she searched in the lower cabinet connected to the bathroom sink for her mom's sanitary products.

Finding nothing, Ari slumped in helpless defeat on the cold, hard floor for a few minutes. She then rose, left out of the bathroom, and headed towards the living room, where her mother sat smoking a cigarette while watching *The Young and The Restless*. Ari learned that it was never a smart thing to interrupt, her mother, while she was watching her soaps. And she learned that lesson the hard way, after successfully dodging a glass ashtray hurled at her one time. Today, she patiently waited until she heard the show take a commercial break. A *Charmin's* tissue commercial allowed her the clearance she needed.

"Momma, I got my period," Ari timidly declared.

"And whatchu tellin' me fo'?" Her mother scoffed as she reached for yet another cigarette. Cigarettes were her vice.

"Where are your sanitary napkins and tampons? I need some," Ari said.

Her mother took two puffs of her new cigarette, never once looking over at her daughter, "You ain't using my stuff. Go get ya own!"

Ari's feelings were hurt. *With what money?*

"I don't have any money, Momma. How am I supposed to get my own?"

"You need to get you a job! That's what you need to do! Laid up all summer doing nothin," she chided before throwing a ten-dollar bill on the table.

Ari hurriedly grabbed the ten-dollar bill and walked out of the house. The sun was blazing and it was terribly humid out. The nearest Walgreens was a nice walk away on 95th and Halsted. She was on 87th and Union.

Because she also wanted snacks to satiate her cravings, she contemplated whether or not she should walk or catch the bus to the store to buy feminine products and something to cure the cramps that were now punching her abdomen like a boxing bag. Despite her pain and the sticky weather that she hated, she decided to walk.

As she traveled down the shaded streets to steer clear of the sun's relentless rays, Ari's heart beat rapidly. At the end of the corner ahead were a few boys from the elementary school she'd just graduated from in June- Marsalis, Trent, Bernard, and Deandre. All of them she despised, especially Marsalis. He was, obnoxious, disrespectful, and brutish. The other three seemed like they would be cool, if they didn't hang out with Marsalis. Ari crossed the street so that she could avoid any form of interactions with these boys. But, of course, the gesture failed. Marsalis saw her and howled like a wolf. The bunch met her right at the end of opposite corner. The same corner she needed to turn on.

"Where you going?" Marsalis asked.

"It's none of your business, so just leave me alone," Ari said and made every effort to sound as if she had an attitude. It didn't work. The boys decided to follow her. She exhaled deeply, swatting Trent's hand as he tried to grab her ponytail that was pulled to the side of her head.

"Ain't you mixed with something? I saw yo momma and she got the same kinda hair as you. What ya'll mixed with- wetback?" Trent goofed. Ari didn't see anything comical about his comment, but obviously Marsalis, Deandre, and Bernard did. They laughed until their faces turned red.

13

"Oh! Would ya look at that! Ari tryin' to grow a booty. She got a booty y'all! Woop woop! Pull over that a-- too fat," Marsalis chanted Trick Daddy's lyrics in between spurts of laughter. He hit Ari on her behind, which excited the other three.

This ordeal was working on her bearings. The tissue that she was using as a panty shield could only last for so long, and she wasn't even on 90th street yet! A headache railroaded her thoughts. Marsalis put his arm around Ari's lower back and whispered into her ear, "Won't you give me yo' number?"

Ari's face read disgust. If Marsalis wasn't so ignorant and mischievous, he may have won her favor. He was the cutest boy in her eighth grade class, but his rude attitude and behavior overshadowed his looks. She was not about to give this demon her number. She scowled at him and tried to turn away from his grasp. Undeterred, Marsalis' green eyes danced with excitement.

"You know I like you. Give me that number and stop playin'," Marsalis cooed, as he tightened his grip.

"I don't like you Marsalis. No," Ari told him with a mean mug.

Deandre, Trent, and Bernard clowned him because he'd been turned down. Marsalis didn't like that. He stuck his foot out and tripped Ari, causing her to fall to her knees. Then, Marsalis kicked her in the butt before she could get back up. The hooligans laughed and ran in the opposite direction as they chanted Trick Daddy's song with Marsalis again. Ari cried.

"You okay?"

Ari looked up to see a browned skinned guy with a friendly face standing over her. He extended his hand and helped her off the ground. She dusted off her brown Capri pants and mumbled, "Yeah... I'm okay."

"My name is Estavian. We went to school together. You remember? You want me to walk you home? I saw what them boys did to you. I don't want them to try and mess with you again," he told her.

Estavian did go to her school, but he'd graduated a few years ago. He was one of those guys she saw frequently around the neighborhood, but she never knew his name. "I'm not going home. I have to go to the st------," Ari started to cry again.

Estavian put his hand on her shoulder, "What's the matter? I thought you said you were ok?"

"You wouldn't understand," she said.

"Hey, maybe I would. I have a younger sister and two older sisters. I probably would understand better than you think. What is it?"

Ari briefly explained her problem and, like Estavian predicted, he knew exactly what she was talking about. He invited her to come over to his house and promised not to try anything funny. Ari didn't know why she trusted him, but it was clear that he was nowhere near as disrespectful as those idiots she'd just encountered. Plus, saving herself a trip to the store that was still blocks away would work in her favor.

"My mom's a nurse too, so she can help you," he said, as they walked across a broad two way street. The side that they were walking towards was considered Stone Terrace or "Stone Tez".

No one from her side of the street went to Stone Tez because of the gang rivalries. Estavian unlocked his front door and called for his mother as he crossed the threshold.

"Ma! I need help with something. Can you come here for a sec?"

Ari stood by the door, just in case she needed to run for some reason. A heavyset woman with light brown micros, wearing scrubs came into the living room where they stood. "What do you want, boy? I'm trying to get ready for work," she said before turning her eyes to Ari.

"And who is she, Estavian?"

"Ma, this is Ari. She needs help with lady stuff," Estavian murmured, somewhat unsure of what to say.

"Lady stuff? Boy, what are you saying?" His mother asked him, confused.

Ari was extremely embarrassed. She wished she'd had some kind of summer job. She would have had the money to buy all the 'lady stuff' she needed for the rest of her life and not have to depend on anybody for anything! But who would hire a thirteen year old?

QUEEN ARI
"... they dug into the creepy crevices where her dark secrets hid."

"It took you that dog on long to go to the sto'?"

That was the first thing Ari heard come from her mother's mouth as she walked inside the house. Running into Estavian turned out to be a blessing for her after all. His mother took her to Walgreens where she bought her everything she needed, including junk food she'd gorged. His mother also gave her tips on how to calculate when her next menstrual would come so that she wouldn't be caught off guard next time. For a moment she felt free and loved. Too bad she had to come home to this.

"You hear me talking to you, you baldheaded rat? Where's my change?"

Ari wasn't sure if it was the heat or her frazzled emotions causing her to tune her mother out and head straight for the kitchen. She hadn't eaten an actual meal in two days because her stale appetite wouldn't allow her. It wasn't like she was missing out on any gourmet cooking though. Everything in the refrigerator was microwavable, and she was so tired of that stupid food. Bile sat at the base of her throat at the thought of even attempting to eat a frozen chicken dinner right now. She closed the refrigerator and met a cold slap to her face from her mother.

"So you can fix yo' mouth to ask me fo' some money to get tampons, but you can't answer me when I ask you a question? Who was you outside with all this time?" Her mother asked with anger piercing through the tiny slits of her eyes. Her hand was ready for another blow as Ari crouched up against the refrigerator with her hand covering her face.

17

"Estavian's momma took me to Walgreens," she yelped.

Her mother's face scrunched up, "Estavian? Who the hell is Estavian? You was with some boy? You 'bout to get it now!"

Her mother wrapped her hand around Ari's long curly ponytail and dragged her on all fours out of the kitchen while she punched Ari in her upper back. Ari hadn't been beat by her mother like this in a few weeks, which was right around the time someone called Child Protective Services on her. Guess she wasn't afraid that she was being watched anymore. Nevertheless, Ari needed to find a way to get loose from this wicked witch.

Despite the frequent beatings, Ari never fought back. In her mind, this was still her mother, her caretaker, the one responsible for her shelter, clothing, and terrible food. How could she fight back? This attack seemed more vicious though, and Ari wasn't sure if this was going to be the last one she'd endure.

With all of her thirteen year old strength, she clawed her fingers into her mother's hand so that she would let go of the vice grip that she had on her hair. She then quickly scrambled up off the floor and surprised herself by retaliating. She punched wildly with no direct target in mind, doing anything she could to cause this beast to retreat.

But it only made her mother even angrier. She charged at Ari and wrapped her hands around her neck. They crashed onto the couch as her mother choked her.

"I can't believe my momma is trying to kill me," Ari thought as she blacked out.

***

"There she is officer! Lock her up. She's pretending like she's hurt. She's a hell of a good actor, I tell ya. Take her to jail," Ari heard her mother shout as she came to.

She rubbed her eyes and saw a light skinned man in uniform standing over her body. Everything was blurry. The only thing she could really make out was the name Anderson on his badge. As she struggled to sit completely upright, her head throbbed and she felt really nauseous.

His voice was very calm, almost fatherly, "Now, we can do this the easy way or the hard way, Ari. Your mother is insisting that we take you to jail. We don't know what it is that you di---"

"The heffa was trying to fight me! That's what she did," her mother cut him off.

"Ari, can you stand up and come with us, please?" Officer Anderson commanded.

Still dizzy and disoriented, she slowly rose to her feet, allowed herself to be handcuffed and taken to the squad car parked outside of her house by Officer Anderson and his female partner. Officer Anderson opened the back door for her, and she wiggled her way inside. The two officers stood outside her home for a few minutes talking to her mother, well listening to her rant and demean her daughter's character. Ari really didn't even care that she was headed to jail. It seemed like a better hell than the place she'd called home. *Why couldn't my life be simple? Why did I have to be born into hate and pain?* These questions caused her to weep. She held her head down, as the tears rolled down her cheeks. After a few more moments, Officer Anderson and his partner got into the car and drove away.

19

"She's crying J.D.," the female officer whispered to her partner, yet it was loud enough for Ari to hear.

"We're not going to take you to jail, Ari. We're going to ride around for a little while so you can tell us what happened between you and your mother," Officer Anderson assured her.

Ari stopped weeping for a bit and looked up confusedly. *Someone wants to hear my story? Would it even matter though?* Her mother always found a way to circumvent all of Ari's attempts to destroy her "perfect mommy" character. Ari felt nauseous again. She kicked those thoughts out of her head momentarily to keep from throwing up. It wouldn't be a good look if she upchucked in this squad car.

"Can we go get something to eat? I can tell you my side, if I can just get something to eat," Ari said.

She was somewhat ashamed to have allowed the little pride she had left to take a leave of absence for that request. She bit her bottom lip and looked out the window.

"Sure we can do that, Ari," Officer Anderson agreed to Ari's surprise.

They drove to a nearby KFC and sat down in the eatery. Ari was so glad to finally be somewhere eating something of quality; it was fast food, but it was way better than what she'd been eating at home. She took a forkful of coleslaw and savored the cold contents in her mouth. It was so good, and so were the barbecue wings and macaroni she'd consumed a few minutes earlier. As she sucked down pink lemonade through the straw, Officer Anderson spoke in the same fatherly tone from earlier, "So, tell me what happened tonight, Ari."

Ari's face turned solemn. She never knew her dad, but she assumed a father-daughter conversation would sound similar to this. She looked over at his female partner. Her badge read Jackson. The soft expression resting on her friendly face looked back at Ari with endearing eyes. Ari then refocused her attention back to Officer Anderson. His eyes were piercing strongly through his glasses, and they dug into the creepy crevices where her dark secrets hid. It didn't even seem like he ever took a moment to blink. Ari wanted to breakdown right then. They had no clue.

QUEEN ARI
"… the tunes of Beethoven's Moonlight Sonata."

<u>September</u>

Ari's face was downcast as she headed to her third week of high school on the CTA. This was the route she would be forced to take now from the motel that they were temporarily staying in. After telling Officer Anderson and Officer Jackson what really happened the night her mother called them to their house, they charged her mother with child abuse and sent Ari to a foster home.

The girls in the foster home were so cruel and mean to Ari that she later recanted the story she told the officers. The charges were dropped against her mother, but a social worker was still assigned to the case when Ari came back home. The frequent visits to their home by the social worker unnerved her mother. To avoid these unwelcomed meetings, she had most of their belongings put in storage while they relocated to a shabby motel, until she found them a new place to live. A source of relief came from her best friend, Evelyn, who always waited at the bus stop for her.

"Hey, sistagirl!"

"Hey, Evey!"

The two hugged each other. They hadn't spoken over the weekend because Evey went away to a poetry retreat. Ari wanted to go too, but her mother refused to pay for it, so she had to stay behind. The girls broke away from their embrace, walked into the school, and placed their book bags on the table to be sent through the metal detector.

"I like your hair, Evey; who did it," Ari asked, admiring the neat cornrow style with honey blonde and brown extensions added to her hair.

"I did it, girl! I learned how to do it while I was in New York. You should let me do yours. You wouldn't even need extensions."

"Yeah? Can you come over my hou—," Ari caught herself. She didn't have a house anymore. She was staying in that dumb motel. Her mother would surely throw her over the balcony if she brought Evey there.

"Huh?" Evey asked.

"Nevermind. How was New York anyway?" Ari asked, changing the subject.

"Oh my God, when we grow up, we got to move there. It's like a bigger, louder Chicago. You know how they call it the city that never sleeps? It's so true! I had so much fun though. I met a lot of cool people too."

"That's good. Did you get to write any new stuff," Ari asked. She always liked the way Evey wrote; it took her to a place other than where she was.

"Girl did I? I will read you some of it during 6th period. See you later, ok?"

"Ok."

The two separated to go to their different classes. Her first period class was American Literature- one of her favorites. Like Evey, she also loved poetry and wrote a lot of stuff but never found a comfortable place to release it anywhere other than in that class. Mr. Raudenbush greeted Ari with a pleasant smile, as she headed to her seat. She was early.

"Hey Ari, how are you this morning?"

"I'm doing good, Mr. Raudenbush. What about you?"

"Oh, basking in the residual ambiance of an eventful weekend similar to the events recounted by Shakespeare's 'Midsummer Night's Dream'," Mr. Raudenbush responded.

Ari's eyes brightened, "Really?"

"Not even close," he laughed.

"Oh," Ari joined his amusement.

He rubbed his hand through his short hair that was as white as snow. His sea blue eyes that hid behind the silver rimmed glasses framing his face twinkled, as he explained to her about his trip to visit his daughter and her husband's side of the family in Michigan. Everyone seemed to have had a pleasant weekend except Ari, better yet a pleasant summer.

His voice trailed away as she daydreamed about being taken to the countryside somewhere far away from here, where there would be mystic mountains, and striking trees with the greenest leaves. Someplace where the wildlife roamed, the people were nice, and the air was fresh.

This was a place where she could be free to be herself. And she wished she could be there with the man she never knew- her father. He would drive her to the local market, and they would buy the best peaches in town. Peaches good enough to make the sweetest peach cobbler. She loved peach cobbler. And at night before bed, she could lie near the fireplace and listen to her father play the piano. He would play the tunes of Beethoven's Moonlight Sonata on the piano, which is actually all the memory she really had of him.

"So how was your weekend Ari?" Unbeknownst to him, Mr. Raudenbush had interrupted an episode in Ari's mind.

"Huh? Oh it was good. Really good," she lied.

***

"I'm so hungry," Evey said rubbing her stomach.

"Me too," Ari replied while standing in line for 6th period lunch. The forty-five minutes they were given for lunch never seemed to be enough, considering almost fifteen minutes were spent waiting in line.

"So what did you get into this weekend, missy?" Evey asked.

"Nothing at all. Wish I could have gotten the money from my mother to go to New York with y'all. I was so bored," Ari said.

"Yeah I bet. Your mother is a different kind of evil, you know that?"

"Tell me about it."

Ari and Evey picked up trays, juice boxes, and fruit cups. Ari looked at the pizza pan as the slices dwindled. "Please don't run out of pizza," she said to herself.

"Oh my God, Ari you won't believe what happened right before 4th period!" Evey exclaimed.

"What?" Ari responded before giggling at Evey's eagerness to tell her something juicy.

The lunch lady put a slice of pizza on Evey's tray, the last slice. Ari groaned. The lady walked away for a few moments. Ari hoped she was going to bring another pan of pizza upfront. No luck; she brought back a pan of chicken patty sandwiches. Ari was beyond disappointed.

"You don't have any more pizza?" She asked the lunch lady.

"Nope. Do you want a chicken patty sandwich?"

Ari shook her head. *How could they run out of pizza?*

"Yeah, I'll take it."

Ari and Evey sat at their usual spot. The lunchroom was huge and carried all the various noises of the students' conversations. 6th period lunch was designated for the freshmen and sophomore students, and 7th period was for the juniors and seniors. A couple weeks ago, Ari skipped her 7th period class to go to lunch, just to get a slice of pizza. It was the first time she'd missed out on pizza in 6th period.

This decision was a mistake. The juniors and seniors were unruly and her plan to sit at an empty table was thwarted after being harassed by the boys on the football team and accosted by the jealous cheerleaders. She ended up eating her pizza in the bathroom to get away from the wolves and hyenas, and to keep from being written up by a security guard for roaming the halls.

"Ok, what happened in 4th period?" Ari asked Evey as she broke a piece of the chicken patty sandwich to eat, only to find it wasn't completely cooked. Disgusted, she pushed her tray to the side and focused her gaze onto her best friend.

"Guess who wants to go with me?" Evey asked breaking her pizza in half before handing Ari one of the halves.

"Thanks, Evey. Who?" She asked, taking a bite.

"Damien."

"Damien who? The football player?"

"Yes! Oh my God! He handed me a note in the hallway right before I went into my class. Let me read you what he wrote." Evey dug in her purse for the note.

"Wait, isn't Damien a senior?" Ari inquired.

"Yeah, so what?" Evey responded, as she continued to rummage through her purse.

"Oooh, a box of Mike and Ikes! Ari, you want some?" Evey offered.

"Yeah. So you're not scared to go with someone who's older than you," Ari asked as she took the box of candies and opened it to take a few in her mouth.

Evey stopped looking for the note and instead applied strawberry Carmax on her lips. "I mean, I thought about that. But then, he's not that old Ari. He's 17 and I'm 13. What's the big deal?"

"He's going to want you to do things," Ari told her.

"Do things? What do you mean 'do things?'" Evey asked with her face scrunched up.

"You know like things," Ari didn't know how else to put it without being totally frank.

"Like sex?" Evey asked innocently.

"Yeah, like in Jason's Lyric, rolling around in the flowers, sex," Ari mused.

Evey laughed. "Noooo, I don't think so."

"Evey, you've accused me of being naïve so many times. I think you're being naïve now. He's going to want to bump and grind with you," Ari then giggled.

The two of them continued to go back and forth with this subject until the first bell sounded, marking the end of 6th period.

The girls got up with the rest of the students to throw away their trash and leave the lunchroom. This part of the day was the best for Ari because she and Evey shared 7th and 8th period together. They walked briskly to their Chemistry class and continued to talk.

"Well, I'll put it this way: if it happens, it happens," Evey said.

Ari gasped and playfully pushed Evey, "You hoochie! I thought you were going to save your virginity until marriage?"

Evey waved her hand at her friend, "Aw come on, Ari. You're so old fashioned. No one waits until marriage anymore."

"I'm going to wait," Ari said.

"Pssssh, please, good luck with that. You just might very well be waiting alone. I'm going to call you Ms. Cobwebs."

The two burst into laughter as they walked into their class. As they sat in their seats, Mr. Christie, their Chemistry teacher, cleared his throat and announced, "Alright, pop quiz."

Evey looked back at the man horrified, "I'm not going to be any good."

"In the bed with Damien or on the test for Mr. Christie," Ari joked.

Evey shook her head smiling, "Oh wow. I so hate you. Shoot, I didn't get a chance to read to you his note!"

QUEEN ARI
"We did the garden roll."

December

"Ari, could you please ask your momma to let you spend the night with me this weekend?" Evey pleaded with Ari over the phone.

"I will. I don't see why she wouldn't. It's Christmas break. Plus she has a new boyfriend-Lonzo. She practically bends over backwards for that bum. But me, I have to beg for a new pair of white K-Swiss," Ari smirked at the thought.

"That's so sad. Well just ask her. I have to tell you something," Evey shared.

"Aw man, what is it?"

"I'm not telling you until you get here. Just let me know if she says yes and I'll ask Estavian to come get you."

"Ok," Ari said before placing the phone on the receiver.

Ari sat in her room going over how she would ask her mother about spending the night out. Her mother rarely let Ari sleep away from home because she claimed that she didn't trust people around her child. Ari, on the other hand, believed her mother didn't want her to find out what a better life was like. Since they moved out of the motel and into a new home, her mother was now very paranoid and extremely overprotective of Ari, as if she truly cherished her.

It was a weird love; one that Ari didn't quite understand. Other than her possessive ways, Ari never heard her mother say "I love you." She never got hugs or kisses from her either, yet she would always see this kind of affection poured into Lonzo.

Her mother would cook big meals for him and buy him clothes. This irritated Ari. She never understood how a grown man could feel so comfortable with taking food out of a child's mouth and how her mother obliged. One thing Ari wasn't too upset about was the fact that the energy used to fuel the random fits of rage she aimed at her was being used on Lonzo. Ari would give Lonzo gratitude for being an inadvertent distraction. Her mother was too head over heels for him, to think about Ari. Yeah, she would most definitely ask to spend the night out, and if she didn't get the answer she was looking for, she would sneak out.

"Momma, can I stay at Evey's this weekend?"

"For what?" Her mother responded while lighting a cigarette.

"We have a project to do together. It's due when we go back in January," Ari lied. Lying had become fairly easy to her and surprisingly she lied well enough to get her way a few good times.

"Damn, they got y'all doing homework over the break? Gone 'head. Before you leave, make sure you let me check your overnight bag."

This was probably the third time she spent the night out and the third time this woman asked to check her bag. She counted Ari's panties, checked for condoms, vibrators, lubrication, pregnancy tests, and pornos.

Ari didn't care though. She knew what she had in her bag and none of it was incriminating, so she could check and count all she wanted. Ari was just happy to get away for a change. She hurriedly ran into the living room to call Evey.

"EVEY! Tell Estavian to come get me!"

***

Estavian blew the horn to his 1995 green two-door Cutlass Supreme. The day Estavian basically came to her rescue in August was also the day Ari became acquainted with Evelyn or Evey for short- his younger sister. Evey didn't attend the same elementary school as her, but she was extremely happy when she found out that they would be going to the same high school. Ari had a few friends from her elementary school, but no one that was as close to her as Evey. Ari loved her like a sister.

Estavian got out of the car, took Ari's bag, and put it in the trunk. He was always so nice to her. Ari had developed a secret crush on him since the first day he helped her. It continued to grow, but he never showed her that he felt the same way. Despite his limited efforts to show her similar interests, she held his images in her mind for her daydreams. He was maturing fairly well, and his playing basketball sculpted his body in a way that made Ari lust for him.

She was attracted to everything about him: from his smooth unblemished caramel skin, to his low haircut with perfect waves, all the way down to how he dressed. He seemed so much more mature than a senior in high school.

31

"So I take it you and Evey are going to keep me up all night with y'all girl talks," he said, while exposing his irresistible Colgate smile.

"You've been able to hear us?" Ari asked, sort of embarrassed. Some of their talks would reach levels that exceeded their level of maturity.

"Yup, you lucky my room is next to Evey's. Y'all would be in big trouble," he said. He laughed after shaking his head.

Ari blushed nervously. Could this mean he knew she liked him? A majority of her parts to the conversations held with Evey were almost always about him, how much she liked him, and how she wondered what it would be like to lose her virginity to him. She didn't even want to look at him right now.

Once they arrived to Evey's home, Ari didn't even wait for Estavian to get out and open the door for her as he usually did. She jumped out of the car and ran straight to the house. But it really didn't matter because he still needed to unlock the door.

"Evey must really got something to tell you huh," he asked her.

"Um, yeah," that was a good excuse for her mad dash.

He shook his head again, "Girls."

***

"I wish I could be as pretty as some of those video girls," Ari told Evey as they watched an episode of 106 & Park, one of the most popular top ten video countdown shows broadcasted on BET.

"Girl please, I don't. I'm happy with how I look," Evey said.

"That's easy for you to say. You *are* pretty like those girls on T.V." Ari told her.

Ari could tell this sort of statement caught Evey off guard. Ari wasn't saying that to be mean. She was just being honest. Evey had the confidence that she herself would have stolen money from her mother to buy, if she knew it were for sale.

She just seemed to grace through puberty. Evey's mother made sure her daughter stayed fly, unlike her own mother. Evey's hair was always done, her complexion was a flawless milky brown, and her clothes fit her body, which was beginning to develop perfectly. As far as Ari was concerned, Evey had no worries to her self-esteem.

"I mean, look at you, Evey, and look at me. No matter what I try to do to my hair, I end up looking like Sideshow Bob from "The Simpsons". My momma buys me a few outfits and one pair of K. Swiss that she thinks should last me for the whole year. Plus, I'm shaped like a boy, and my face breaks out when the wind changes directions. I can't compete with you," Ari vented.

Evey's eyebrows furrowed, "Who said we were competing against each other? I thought we were sisters?"

When Evey said this, Ari felt bad. She cried. Evey wrapped her arm around Ari. Later on that day, after their pizza was delivered, Evey sorted through her closet and gave Ari some of her nicest clothes. She made Ari pretend that she was at a spa and gave her a cucumber facial, washed and blow-dried Ari's hair and put neatly styled cornrows in it.

"Ta daaaaa," Evey exclaimed after she was finished.

Ari beamed while looking into the mirror. She liked her new hairdo, "Thanks Evey!"

"Can you see how beautiful you are now?" Evey asked.

"I guess. So all this time I've been here, why haven't you told me that thing you needed to tell me?"

"Oh shoot! I forgot but I didn't forget."

Evey sat in her bed and left Ari sitting at the vanity. Ari turned around to face her friend and said, "Soooo..."

"Weeeeell, It's about me and Damien."

Ari's eyes bulged, "What about you and Damien?"

Evey paused for a minute then blushed, "We did it."

"Did what?"

"Oh so now you're going to be slow, Ari? We did the garden roll."

Ari covered her face and gushed, "I can't believe it! Oh my God! I should have known!"

"I told you if it happened it would happen," Evey shrugged.

"So give me the details. How did it feel? Did it hurt?"

QUEEN ARI
"Her heart thumped when she thought of the gift …"

"Please, Ari! Can you just cover for me this one time? It's not like I've ever left you before. I just want to see my Boo for a minute," Evey begged.

"No! Why would you invite me over here if you knew you were going to see Damien?"

"I didn't know he was going to want to see me tonight! Please, Ari? Pretty pleeeaaase?"

Ari sighed, "Alright! You're lucky your momma is working the night shift tonight or else I would have said no and just let you get in trouble."

"You wouldn't have. Ok, I promise I will be back. Don't go to sleep, ok," Evey said, as Ari walked with her to the front door to see her out. Once she locked the door, she walked back upstairs to Evey's room and was scared senseless when she bumped into Estavian.

She clutched her chest and gasped, "Oooh, you scared the mess out of me!"

"My bad," he said.

"Why are you still up?" She asked him.

"I don't know. I couldn't sleep, thought I heard noises downstairs."

"Aw, that was me. I, I was thirsty," Ari made up.

"Aw ok."

Estavian made an about face and headed back to his room. Ari walked slowly behind him. She sort of was hoping he would invite her into is room. For what, she didn't know.

To her surprise, he went into the bathroom across the hall. His T.V. blasted the beginning lyrics of Donell Jones singing, "Where I Wanna Be". Ari stood at the door bobbing and singing along. Estavian scared her again by poking her in the side,

"This yo' song?"

She cooed a little, "Maybe."

She stayed at the door, until she got the much anticipated invitation from him, "You can come in if you want."

"Close the door," he told her and she did.

She sat in bed with him as they watched the night's episode of Midnight Love, which showed nothing but the best R&B videos, old and new.

"Evey did your hair?" Estavian asked.

"Yeah," she responded.

He said nothing else as he changed the channel once the final video played out. He turned it over to "Sanford and Son." Ari laughed, "You're an old man."

"Why? Because I like Sanford and Son?"

"Yeah." Ari poked fun.

"Well you're watching it with me so that makes you an old lady."

"Uh uh. I turned 14 in September but I'm still young enough to get away with it,' she giggled.

"Is that right? So what can I get away with then?" He looked over at her with a grin.

She shrugged sheepishly, "I don't know."

Estavian turned the volume down on the T.V. and looked back over at Ari with a serious expression. His dark eyes locked on her.

She wanted to look away at something else, but the room was completely dark, minus the light from the T.V. He moved in closer to her, and Ari's heart beat rapidly.

What's happening? Oh my God, what's happening?

Estavian partially licked his lips, leaned toward Ari and kissed her slightly.

"I like you, Ari."

Ari couldn't talk. He stole her words.

"I've always liked you," he continued and then kissed her again.

He gently pushed her down on his bed and caressed her small frame. He nibbled on her neck and it tickled her. She felt his hands creep down her body. Her sharp exhales cut his face.

Ari constantly replayed this fantasy in her head as she lay in bed waiting on Evey to come home. She wondered if this would have actually happened had she accepted Estavian's invitation to come into his room to watch the rest of Midnight Love.

***

The weekend at Evey's passed by too fast. The next thing Ari knew, she was in the car with Estavian heading back home, someplace she wished she didn't have to return to. Missy Elliot's "Hot Boyz" was playing on WGCI as they headed back to her side of town.

"I like your hair like that Ari," Estavian said, breaking the silence.

"Thanks," Ari responded blushing. She stared out the window, contemplating whether or not she should tell him about her crush on him.

If she told him and he didn't feel the same way or even worse, laughed at her, she would be devastated. She kept her mouth closed.

"So when are you going to come back over to spend the night again?" Estavian asked.

Ari couldn't help but jump off her gitty caboose when she heard his question.

"Um, I don't know. My mom's pretty strict about me spending the night out a lot."

"Well if you can't make it on or before Christmas…" He paused as he parked in front of Ari's home. He reached into the glove compartment and pulled out a small gift bag.

"I wanted to give you this," Estavian said, handing her the bag.

She slowly took the bag from him and peeked inside. A gift wrapped rectangle box sat at its bottom. Her heart burst with excitement. She'd never been given a gift before, especially not from a boy.

"You got this for me?"

"Yeah," he responded in a somewhat shy manner.

Ari beamed, "Thank you."

"Now you have to promise me that you won't open it until the clock strikes twelve, Christmas Day, okay?"

Ari could care less about his instructions. She was in love with a gift she hadn't opened yet from a boy she now assumed liked her as much she liked him. Could that latter part of her thinking be too farfetched? He got out the car and took her overnight bag out of the trunk, then opened the door for her. Tiny snowflakes started to fall. This would be the first fall of snow for the winter season.

"You promise?" Estavian asked as he handed over her overnight bag.

Ari gave him one of her most radiant smiles ever, "Yeah, I promise."

Estavian pinched her cheek and smiled back at her, "A'ight, Beauty. I'm going to hold you to that. See you later."

After telling him goodbye and watching him drive off, she stood at her door for a while, dreading going inside. She was greeted by Lonzo when she finally walked in. Ari thought he was an obnoxious Neanderthal. She hated his scent- asphalt and dry wall. She hated his construction jumpsuit that he always wore. She hated his shifty hazel eyes and potbelly that was filled with the meals that her mother never offered her. She hated his dirty nails and fat pink fingers that resembled Vienna sausages. She hated the gold tooth that replaced one of his K9's. And most of all, she hated how much her mother loved him.

"Hey," she spoke dryly.

'What's in the bag?" Lonzo asked.

"Nothing,"

"So you got you a lil' nigga buying you gifts huh," he said, chewing on a toothpick.

"No one's buying me gifts," Ari responded sharply. She didn't like his reference for Estavian.

"Yeah, a'ight. I saw him drop you off."

"So what," Ari said, running up the stairs and straight to her room. She had a hard time listening to someone she didn't respect.

She hurriedly hid her gift from Estavian in her closet and emptied out her clothes, including the one's Evey gave her this weekend. As she hung the garments up, her bedroom door burst open.

"What's this about some boy dropping you off? That's where you were this whole weekend huh? That's where you were?" Her mother's voice was high pitched and frantic.

"No! That was Evey's brother. He's the one that picks me up and drops me off, momma."

Ari was terrified. This spelled a beat down in every language.

"You think I'm dumb don't you! Pull ya pants down!"

Ari's eyes almost popped out of their sockets, "Waaa—what?"

"I said, pulled ya doggone pants down! Now!"

Ari reluctantly unbuttoned her pants as her mother went to close the door. She came back staring her dead in the face. Obviously irritated by the amount of time it took for Ari to comply with her command she grabbed her daughter's pants and pulled her panties down with them.

"Now spread your legs."

"What for momma?"

"I said...spread...your...legs...,"her mother grunted.

Ari had never felt so humiliated in her life. She stepped out of her bottoms and stood still, not knowing what was next. Her mother crouched down and examined her private area. Ari closed her eyes as she allowed her mother to perform a cavity search on her to look for whatever she thought could prove she was sexually active.

"You must think, I'm Boo Boo the fool. Don't ever ask me to spend the night over Evey's house again. You lucky I didn't find anything. You would be one dead..."

The end of her mother's rant was a word Ari was glad was muzzled by the door. Shocked and mortified, she sat down on her bed and stared at the wall in front of her. It turned into a window where she was able to see herself happy and free.

She was walking hand in hand with Estavian. She was laughing uncontrollably, as he spun her around. All she really wanted was to be loved and not despised, wanted and not rejected, hugged and not beaten. Why did her father leave her here with this woman? Was it because he didn't love her either?

"And take them cornrows out yo' head. You look like an ugly boy!"

Her mother had managed to break the imaginary window on her wall by kicking her confidence in the stomach. She got up from her bed and put her clothes back on. She then went into the bathroom to take the cornrows down. She could barely make out her reflection, since a sea of salted tears blocked her vision.

Once the last braid was taken down, she stared into the mirror, trying hard to see what made her so unattractive. Though this was not the first time her appearance had taken a jab, she tried hard to understand how she didn't look like her mother, who would be considered a gorgeous woman if she weren't so evil. How would Ari ever be able to find the beauty in herself if, with every chance she got, her mother found a way to throw dirt on it? Why wasn't she strong enough to protect this beauty?

***

"A'ight, I'm going to work. Make sure you wash them dishes, take out the trash, and do the last of that laundry. And I can tell how long you be on my phone, so don't think you gone use up today by talking to yo lil friends either. Let me come home from work and find my house is still nasty; I'ma beat yo tail raw!"

This was Ari's so called wakeup call from her mother. She looked over at her alarm clock. 7:08 a.m. Might as well get up and do what she was told so she wouldn't have to worry about it later. She stretched as a yawn pushed itself out of her. After jumping out of bed, she went into the closet to get her house shoes. Ari caught a glimpse of the gift bag Estavian gave her yesterday and reached inside to run her fingers over the neatly wrapped box. Christmas was just a few days away, but Ari wished it was sooner so she could open it.

She went into the bathroom, brushed her teeth, and washed her face. As she dried her face, a noise from downstairs startled her. She placed the towel back in its place and ran downstairs. To her horror, Lonzo was sitting in the living room watching T.V. and eating a huge bowl of cereal. *Why is he even here?*

"What up Baby girl," he spoke with a mouthful of cereal.

Ari grimaced, "Hey."

Since she would have to clean up the kitchen anyway, she decided to tackle that chore first. She cleaned out the refrigerator, cleaned the stove, washed the dishes, swept, and mopped the floor. Before she could leave the kitchen, Lonzo came in and threw his bowl and spoon into the sink.

"Wash that for me will, ya," he said then belched.

"I hate you, you stupid dog," Ari said under her breath. She meant every word.

Normally, Ari really didn't have a problem doing her chores but today was different because Lonzo was there. He deliberately did things to get in her way. It took her longer to finish than it would have if he were gone somewhere else.

Despite the inconveniences Lonzo created, every task was completed by 10:30 that morning. She exhaled a sigh of relief, as she sat down at the computer desk in the dining room. Ari used the Internet to communicate with Evey since her mother wasn't too versed on Internet chatting.

"Did you ask me for permission to get on the computer?" Lonzo asked walking in the dining room.

"No. What for?" Ari retorted not really even paying him any attention.

"I bought that computer. You supposed to ask me for permission," he responded.

"I don't have to ask you for anything. You're not my father. You don't have any authority over me," Ari shot back.

She heard him leave out of the dining room and come back. Her back was to him. She turned around and dug her eyes into his face.

"What? What are you standing there for? I'm not going to ask you for permission to use anything in this house, so you can just go back into the living room and watch "The Price Is Right" or whatever you were watching, you sloppy idiot!"

Ari hated this man with every inch of her being, and she didn't care that he knew it. As soon as she turned back around to face the computer, Lonzo rushed towards her and put her in a chokehold. He pulled her out of the chair that flipped over from the commotion.

"I'm 'bout to make you into a woman, and I'm not gone ask permission. How about that," he said as he dragged her upstairs.

Ari had never been this afraid. She couldn't breathe. This man was about to rape her, and she couldn't find the strength to fight him. He was so much stronger than her mother. He flung her into her bed. As she tried to run towards her window, he grabbed her leg and pulled her back towards him. He slapped her across the face. The blow shocked Ari's skin.

"And you gotta smart mouth, I'ma show you how to use it," he said.

He unzipped his pants and forced her legs open. Ari screamed as he pressed all of his 215 lbs on top of her, nearly squeezing the breath out of her. He struggled to pull down her pajama pants and underwear but he managed to overpower her and get them off. She was completely exposed to him. Lonzo started to kiss and bite on her neck. Ari cried and pleaded with him. But he cared little, as he took his member and tried to force himself inside of her.

This can't be happening. God, please don't let him do this to me!

Lonzo was unable to get Ari's treasure to accept him. He licked his right hand and put it on her jewel. Ari used that small moment to knee him something vicious in the area he was going to use to violate her. He shrieked in pain. She got up, grabbed her clothes, ran straight downstairs, and out of the house.

It was freezing outside but it didn't matter to Ari. She walked down her block and felt her nose running. She wiped it to see blood. She walked about a mile to get to Evey's house. Once there, she ran up the stairs ringing the doorbell in a panic. Evey came to the door surprised.

"Ari, wha---…"

"Please let me come in. Please!"

Ari told Evey everything that had transpired. But she made her promise not to tell anyone. She stayed over Evey's until she knew her mother would be home. Evey's mom dropped her off back at home and watched as she rang the doorbell. No one answered.

Sort of relieved she walked over and pulled out the spare key from underneath one of the flowerpots sitting on the porch and let herself inside. She waved to Evey's mom before she closed the door. She ran straight to her room and closed the door. Her room was torn apart, as well as her closet.

Her heart thumped when she thought of the gift Estavian gave her. The gift bag had been ripped and strewn about with the tissue paper. Icy tears blocked her visual as she searched through her closet until she found the rectangular box.

No longer in the mood to wait until Christmas Day to open it, she peeled the wrapping paper, raised the lid, and found a gold necklace with the letter "A" dangling as its pendant. She wiped her face before she put the necklace on and held on to the small medallion. At that moment, Ari decided that this necklace would serve as a reminder to hold onto whatever made her beautiful, no matter what.

QUEEN ARI

"The fire within her blazed on the eve of this new-year."

"So what's your plans for tonight?"

"Being imprisoned in this hellhole."

"You don't think your mom will let you come over here?"

"Nope. She said I will never be allowed to spend the night at your house as long as I'm living under her roof."

"She's so unfair. I'm sorry, but I can't stand your baldheaded mother! When are you going to tell her about what her trifling boyfriend did to you?"

Ari clenched her fists. She sat at the computer contemplating how to respond to Evey, whom she was conversing with online. Anger rose up from the pit of her belly. She couldn't believe Lonzo had the audacity to attack her and yet still feel free to come around as if nothing ever happened. He had no shame. And she had no courage to tell her mother what he tried to do. In her mind, her mother was just as guilty as Lonzo. Her mother would never defend her.

"No I didn't. I sort of feel like she's going to take his side anyway," she typed.

"Right. But what if he tries to attack you again Ari? I don't think you're safe there as long as he continues to come around."

"If he tries again, I'm going to kill him!"

"You get off that damn computer. You been on it for hours! Go read a book or something," her mother yelled as she walked past to go to the kitchen.

"I gotta go Evey. I will talk to you later when these demons drink themselves into a temporary pit."

"Okay girl. I love you Sista!"

"Love you too Girly!"

Ari logged out of the computer and went into the kitchen where her mother still was. She stood there for a moment watching her mother search through the refrigerator.

"Where my beer at? That fool done drank all my stuff and ain't said nothin' 'bout it," she mumbled to herself.

Ari wondered how much more alcohol was her mother going to consume tonight. She as well as Lonzo, were already drunk. Ari let out an exasperated sigh. She just wanted her bag of cherries and apple juice.

"What? Whatchu just huff fo'? You got some kind of attitude or something? You been smellin' yo'self a lot lately. Don't…don't make me have to break a broom over yo back," her mother stammered slamming the door to the refrigerator.

Her eyes were glassy and soulless and her face was flushed red. Evidence that she needed not another drink. She walked out of the kitchen yelling Lonzo's name.

The days prior to tonight, Ari's private resentment towards her mother and her inability to confront her about the pervert she loved showed up as public defiance and rebellion. She talked back to her more and bucked up when her mother threatened to beat her a new name. She had no remorse about it either. The fire within her blazed on the eve of this new-year.

After taking the bag of cherries and apple juice out of the refrigerator, she went upstairs to her room and turned on her T.V. switching channels until she found something entertaining to watch. VH1 was showing highlights of the year with celebrity news and videos. After a while, Ari dozed off.

***

"Ye' though you walk through the valley of the shadow of death, you shall fear no evil. I'm protecting and leading you. Don't be afraid. Be bold. Be courageous! I am always with you. I am always with you."

Ari heard a male voice say.

"Is that you daddy? Daddy is that you? Come get me. I want to be with you! I don't want to be here! Come get me daddy! Please," she cried out to the voice.

She frantically looked around for the man that was speaking until she noticed she was on a merry-go-round. She held on tightly to the animal she was sitting onto; a unicorn. The lights of the merry-go-round were blinding which caused her to squint. A familiar classical tune played as she tried to make sense of where she was exactly.

"Daddy, answer me! Why won't you come get me? Why do you have me here? I want to be with you! Take me with you," she implored.

"I am with you, Ari. I am always with you. You don't have to look for me. I am already here. Did you hear me Ari? Did you hear me?"

"Wait, what did you say?" Ari asked.

The lights of the merry-go-round shut off and it stopped moving. Ari blinked many times before she realized she was in her bed looking up at the ceiling. It was all a dream.

49

"I said did you hear me?"

Ari rose up from her bed to see Lonzo standing at her door.

"So you gone act like you ain't hear me when I was calling you huh?" He poked.

Ari gave him a look as if she smelled something foul. She could have sworn she'd locked her door. Him standing slightly in her room proved her wrong.

"What do you want Lonzo?"

"I'm finna run to the sto' to get me and ya momma some more beer. You want somethin'?"

"I don't.' Ari replied.

Lonzo continued to stand by her door. She didn't understand why, since she'd already answered his question. Her bladder was full of apple juice. She got up her from her bed and walked towards the door to go to the bathroom.

"Where you bout to go?" He asked her.

"Um, none of your business. Can you move out of my way, please?"

Ari looked him in his face. His hazel eyes were bloodshot red. The pink mole above his lip made Ari gag. She pushed him in his chest, "I have to use the bathroom. Move out of my way!"

Lonzo grabbed Ari's wrist and twisted her arm behind her.

"You know I never got to finish where we started," he whispered.

"Why are you whispering Lonzo? You don't want my mother to know you up here harassing me? Mom---."

Ari attempted to scream for her mother but Lonzo put his hand over her mouth. He still had her arm twisted behind her as he led her into the room. He kicked the door closed with his feet. Ari allowed him to manhandle her because she had a plan for him.

"Aw so you ready huh? You not gone fight me?" He asked grinning devilishly.

He unzipped his pants and Ari pulled out her pepper spray and a butcher knife. She sprayed him in the face and slashed his arm with the knife. Lonzo flailed and called her out of her name as he rubbed his eyes. Ari jumped up from her bed and begin to punch him wildly.

"Get the hell out of my room!!! Get out of here! Get out!" She screamed.

He tried to fend her off and realized his arm was leaking. He swung at her but missed and staggered out of the room. Ari ran out behind him but went straight to go to the bathroom or else she would have ruined her clean panties.

As she sat on the toilet she heard her mother screaming, "What happened to you? Why you bleeding? Baby what happened to yo arm?"

"Yo' crazy daughter cut me! I just went up there to ask if she wanted something from the sto' and she cut me. That broad is crazy! I'm going home I can't stay here with that disrespectful trick of yours. You need to put her in check," he yelled.

"You lying devil," Ari spoke under her breath.

Shortly after, Ari heard the front door of the house slam.

Once she completely relieved herself, she flushed the toilet and washed her hands. When she opened the door of the bathroom she was startled to see her mother standing there with an angry expression. She backhanded Ari in the face.

"You stupid wench!"

Ari pushed her mother aside who was still drunk and ran into her room locking it behind her.

Her mother kicked and banged on the door as the clock struck 12 o'clock midnight.

Ari sat on her bed as the sound of fireworks harmonized with her mother's violent confrontation with the door. Ari was just relieved the door was receiving the attack and not her this time around.

"Daddy, I wish I was with you. Happy New-Year…"

QUEEN ARI
"...one can never know what someone has gone through based upon his/her appearance."

April 2004

"Ari, have you decided what color you're going to wear for prom?"

"Nope, maybe blue or pink. I don't know. I'm still undecided," Ari told Evey, as they walked around Ford City Mall.

Senior year would be ending soon and Ari couldn't be more excited. Her four years in high school were not hell, but they did come with their typical guns and roses. She was deathly introverted and too insecure to ever fit in with the popular crowds, and she couldn't tread below the radar to fit in with the nerds; thanks to her association with Evey, who was the complete opposite. Evey didn't join the cheerleading squad because neither one of them liked those girls, but she did, however, become a majorette with the school's band, which pushed her into the spotlight just a little.

Ari, on the other hand, decided to excel in academics and the arts. She joined the Beta club and the National Honors Society, where she felt at home. With the help of Mr. Raudenbush, whom she kept in contact with, she managed to snag a literary grant for college. Senior year, she admitted, seemed to be a cool breeze for her, minus the fact that her mother had yet to give her money for senior fees or for her prom dress and accessories.

After that incident between Ari and Lonzo on New Year's Eve in 2000, he came around every blue moon. Her mother blamed Ari even though Ari never told her what really happened to lead up to that incident. She didn't put her hands on her as much, but she still found ways to get back at her. She held onto this grudge even as Ari made it to her senior year.

"Girl what are you waiting for? Prom is just around the corner you know. My mom found my dress online. It should be here next week. I can't wait to try it on," Evey said excited.

"It would help if my mom would stop promising to give me money for my stuff and actually do it," Ari sighed.

"I know, right," Evey replied.

"Oh! Guess what, Ari?"

"What?"

"Estavian is coming up next weekend for my birthday!"

Ari's eyes lit up. The butterflies in her stomach fluttered wildly. She and Estavian became close but not close enough for Ari. One reason was that her mother kept a tight leash on her after she found out about Estavian four years ago. She wouldn't allow her to spend the night out, she monitored her calls, and she put Ari on a strict curfew.

Ari and Estavian wrote each other to keep in touch, especially while he was away in school. But the letters soon stopped after a couple of months. Ari assumed he'd found a girlfriend. She did, however, continue to wear the gold necklace with her first initial as a charm that he gifted her before Christmas. Somehow, she held out hope that he would come back for her; what a perfect fairytale that would be.

"Did you hear me Ari?"

"Yeah, I heard you," Ari responded after sedating those pesky butterflies.

***

"What do you mean, momma?"

"When I got off the boat, my car was gone. They took the car to the impound lot! I had to use the money for yo' prom stuff to get my car back!"

Nothing her mother was saying over the phone was registering. Prom was a week away now. She couldn't have possibly spent the money for her prom dress. Matter of fact, that story didn't sound believable at all. *If I did the math, I'd say you gambled it away!*

"How could you? How am I supposed to go on prom without a dress? I should have known you were going to do something to keep me from going on prom! You never want to see me happy," Ari spoke through disappointment.

She could hear her mother sniffling. She rarely ever heard or saw her mother cry. The troll was expressing another emotion other than rage for a change. Ari almost felt sorry for her, but the pity for her mother quickly faded when she thought about not being able to go on prom. To make it worse, Evey took it upon herself to tell Estavian that Ari didn't have a date for prom. *Now, what am I going to do? My life is done for.*

"I can try and see if Lonzo can get me the money. We can probably get some of it back. We can—."

The fact that she felt that Lonzo would be a profitable alternative was revolting.

"Momma, I don't even want to hear it," Ari said before slamming the phone down on the receiver.

Ari sat in the dark dining room. The was no noise in the room, minus the soft thumps of her tears landing on the plastic placemat. How could her mother be so irresponsible and inconsiderate? She promised herself that when she had children of her own, she would never put them through so much pain and frustration.

***

"Alright class, now that the semester is over and you all will be graduating in a few weeks, you can take your art portfolios with you," Mrs. Akigbe told Ari's class.

5th period Art class was another one of her favorite classes but unfortunately, it wasn't giving her the solace she needed today. She got out of her seat and cleaned up her area, as the rest of her class carelessly did the same.

"Ari before you leave the class, I need to speak to you for a few minutes," Mrs. Akigbe said.

Ari sighed. Mrs. Akigbe was nice, but she didn't feel like being bothered. *Why does she need to talk to me?* Ari waited until everyone cleared away from the drawers where all the portfolios were held. When the crowd dispersed and left the class, she searched through the drawer for her portfolio but couldn't find it.

"Mrs. Akigbe, do you know where my art portfolio is?"

"It should be in the drawer where the others were. You don't see yours, Sweetie?"

"No. I don't see it. I've looked in all the drawers."

Ari looked for her portfolio with trepidation. She really cherished the work she'd created and now it was looking like she'd be leaving out of the class with nothing to show for her efforts. She was furious.

"Maybe someone took it by accident, Ari. They may come back later. Come back here before you leave school," Mrs. Akigbe said.

"Ari, is this yours?" A familiar voice asked.

Ari looked towards the door from where the voice came. It was Evey holding what looked like wet garbage. She hesitantly walked in that direction. Evey was holding remnants of Ari's portfolio in her hands. Ari's breathing was jagged as she slowly took the wet mess out of her best friend's hands.

"Oh nooo," Mrs. Akigbe's muffled laments seemed to have traveled around the classroom and hit Ari upside the head, pushing her back into reality.

She walked to the garbage can and looked over inside to find her entire portfolio had been tossed in with the rest of the trash. It would have been saved had a bottle of juice that was tossed inside had not been opened which wasted all over her work. She shrugged her shoulders and shook her head. Her tears were held hostage by irritation and dismay. She snatched all of the contents from Evey's hands, threw them in the garbage can and ran to the bathroom. Evey followed her.

In the bathroom, she kicked the wall and screamed, "I hate my life! I hate my life! I want to die!"

Evey stood by silently near one of the sinks. Ari breathed heavily and was surprised her eyes hadn't produced any tears. Had she run out of them?

Mrs. Akigbe came into the bathroom with the girls. Her African accent sounded somewhat melodious, "I'm so sorry, my sweet Ari. I'm so sorry."

Ari was so tired of crying. She was so tired of things not working in her favor. She was so tired of getting the short end of the stick. Mrs. Akigbe walked up to Ari, and she collapsed into her teacher's open arms. After holding Ari in a tight embrace for a few moments, Mrs. Akigbe grabbed her hand and led the girls back into her art classroom, where Ari released all of her frustrations. She hadn't even told Evey some of the things she shared, which came as an unpleasant surprise to her best friend. They stayed in that class until school was over because Mrs. Akigbe insisted upon helping to resolve Ari's unfortunate circumstances. After the last bell, Mrs. Akigbe gathered her belongings and asked the girls to accompany her to her car. She drove to a boutique close to the school and helped Ari find a dress, shoes, and accessories for prom.

Ari tried on the dress and stared at her reflection in the mirror before walking out of the fitting room to show Mrs. Akigbe and Evey how well it fit. It was an orange, haltered top dress, with beaded designs that trailed from the top of the dress around to the back. It was beautiful and served as the perfect complement to Ari's style and features. The shoes she found were gold and sparkled just as vividly as the chandelier earrings Evey selected. After a final glance, she took a deep breath and walked out of the fitting room to meet her teacher and her best friend.

"My Ari, you look beautiful. Are you pleased with this dress?" Mrs. Akigbe asked.

"I am," Ari responded, mesmerized by the image of herself. She couldn't remember the last time she looked at her reflection for so long.

"I think orange should be your favorite color Ari. You look really pretty in it," Evey complimented.

Mrs. Akigbe bought all of Ari's things for prom. Once they left the boutique, she took the girls out to Famous Dave's to get something to eat.

"Are you feeling better now, Ari?" Mrs. Akigbe asked.

"Yeah. Much better. I really can't thank you enough, Mrs. Akigbe. I'm super excited about prom. I can't wait," she said.

"Ari, my mom can do your hair and makeup," Evey told her.

She had never been this happy in her entire life. While they ate, Mrs. Akigbe told them about her childhood and what it was like growing up in Somalia, her native land: At the age of 12, she was taken by her mother, auntie, and grandmother, to a circumciser in their village, where she underwent a procedure to have part of her clitoris and her inner labia removed. Ari and Evey couldn't believe what they were hearing.

Moreover, they didn't understand why the women agreed to this procedure. After she married and became pregnant with a girl, she convinced her husband to come to America so that she wouldn't have to worry about being pressured to put her daughter through the same thing. She was fortunate because he agreed, and even more fortunate to deliver her baby without complication, unlike so many other women who went through the same "procedure"

As she listened to the story, Ari developed a new appreciation for Mrs. Akigbe. She seemed so strong and confident. Her beautiful dark brown face always carried happiness and peace. In that moment, Ari realized that one can never know what someone has gone through based upon his/her appearance. She vowed to accept this truth from then on. She was truly grateful to have met someone like Mrs. Akigbe.

QUEEN ARI
"Can your pain compare to this?"

The butterflies in Ari's stomach were dancing, and they felt like they were about to burst out of her when the doorbell rang. She admired her hair that was styled in a neat pin up with the back pressed out. She made sure her makeup was still flawless before going down to the door.

"Ari, I think that's your date!" Her mother shouted from downstairs.

It was time for prom. Today truly felt like a fairytale as she walked down the stairs, and it couldn't have gone any better. Surprisingly, her mother didn't do anything to mess it up. She was actually very helpful.

Estavian looked just as handsome as ever in his white tux, orange tie, and matching shoes. In his hands, he held a white carnation that would be her corsage. He took her wrist and slid the ornament on with ease.

"You're beautiful, Ari," he softly whispered.

Nothing could mess up this day. Not even the scratchy throat that was signaling she was trying to catch a cold could come between Ari and this moment of total bliss. Estavian politely led her to the passenger side of the white Cadillac CTS that was parked outside of her house and allowed her to get in. She gazed back at him as she settled into her seat. He hadn't changed a bit since the last time she'd seen him, and she was grateful for that.

Prom was held at the Marriot hotel on Michigan Avenue in downtown Chicago. Ari ended up being the envy of her class, since word quickly spread that her date was in college.

Of course, she could care less; she just wanted to have fun and that is exactly what she did. After hours of eating, dancing, and taking a host of pictures, it was time for this lovely day to come to a close.

"Did you enjoy yourself, Ari?" Estavian asked.

"I really did. I'm glad you were my date too,' Ari bashfully admitted, while trying not to make eye contact.

Estavian smirked, "Do you have a curfew?"

"I do, but my mother didn't mention it today. Guess she didn't want to bother me."

"Oh, ok. Well, do you want to stay with me for a while?"

Before Ari could say anything, she restrained her gleefulness. She didn't want to come off as too eager. But who was she fooling? She wanted to stay with him forever! Not just a little while.

"Sure, I would like that."

They drove to the south loop and parked in front of a loft. Estavian helped Ari out of the car and into the mini palace. She was in awe. The ceilings were high and the furniture was modern and fresh. The closest she'd been to seeing something like this was when she watched the home design show on the HGTV network.

"Whose place is this?"

"My mentor's. He gave me a spare key and told me I could come by here whenever I came back from school and just wanted to get away. You like it?"

"I do. I really do. I want something like this," Ari said while gazing at the huge paintings on the walls and African artifacts in their various places throughout the loft.

"When I graduate, I'm going to buy this place for us," Estavian said.

Confused, Ari turned around and looked at him, "For us or for you?"

"For us. I'm going to marry you, Ari," Estavian said and walked off.

"Whatever. You don't want to marry me. You already have somebody for that," she said, while she followed him into the kitchen.

"Not even. I've had girlfriends but none of them compared to you."

It was weird that he was telling her this after all this time. She coughed and cleared her throat. That scratchy feeling was getting on her last nerve.

"Why did you stop writing me?" She asked him.

"I never stopped writing you. You stopped writing me. I was glad when Evey said you didn't have a date for prom. I had an excuse to see you. I thought you were mad at me or something."

What? She couldn't believe it. What happened to the letters she'd never received? She would ask her mother once she got home. Estavian handed her a cup of orange juice.

"You must be getting sick, Ari. Sorry, I don't have any medicine for you. But yeah, as soon as I finish school, I'm going to take you away and make you my wife. How does that sound?"

Ari just stared at him. Where was all of this coming from? She did recall him hinting around to this in some of their letters. Honestly, since she wasn't hearing from him anymore, she forced herself to forget his promises. This was like a dream come true, however. There was so much she wanted to tell him though.

"That's ok I will show you, watch," Estavian said, then laughed.

"Come on; let's go to bed," he insisted.

Ari took his hand, as he led her up some stairs. A headache threatened her night of peaceful rest. She sneezed a few times.

"Po' baby," Estavian said.

He pulled a long T-shirt out of the closet for her to sleep in. She took it and went into the bathroom. She really didn't want to take off her dress. It was so pretty, especially since she had some developing curves. Once completely in her nightwear, she nervously stepped out of the bathroom and into the bedroom.

She almost passed out upon seeing Estavian without his shirt. He must have been working out while away because she surely didn't remember him being so buff. He turned around and smiled. "What's the matter?"

"Nuh—nothing."

"Come here."

Ari slowly walked over and climbed in the bed. He pulled her close to him. His entire scent made her melt. She felt a strange sense of security while lying in his arms. She could have stayed for eternity. She wondered if he wanted her in the way a man would. She looked up at him and surprised herself by giving him a kiss on the cheek.

He smirked once again, "You're so precious, Ari."

"You're going to catch my cold," she told him.

"So."

He lifted her face up to his by her chin and kissed her delicately. Ari had never kissed anybody. Fire fueled by all kinds of foreign feelings engulfed her insides.

Estavian slowly let go of his hold of her and positioned himself on top of her. His kisses turned a little more aggressive. He nibbled on her neck, slightly tickling her, so she giggled a little. She felt like the typical immature virgin.

Estavian placed one of his hands on her treasure trough, as he nibbled on her ear. That gesture also made Ari laugh. This time, he joined her amusement. He continued to kiss and suck on her neck.

"Can I have you, Ari," he asked her softly.

"Ye---yeah."

Did I just tell him yes? Oh my God! Her heart was beating like someone playing the Conga drums. Sweat traveled from her collarbone down to her cleavage. The thought of finally losing her virginity to the man she'd made love to a hundred times in her daydreams made her nervous. But it was too late to renege now. She'd just said yes. After unclothing, he used protection before entering Ari's garden and they made love.

Their night of passion initiated a relationship that Ari was completely invested in. Estavian gave her all of the attention she'd always wanted from a male figure. She loved him with her entire life. It was a blissful summer romance indeed and Ari convinced herself that she would strive for its longevity. Unfortunately, this did not make her mother happy. They fought almost every day. It only made matters worse when Ari informed her she would be living on campus at Columbia. She managed to get scholarships and grants for school, but she still needed things for her dorm life that her mother refused to supply. It was a few weeks before Ari was scheduled to move into the dorms, when she decided that this would be the last time she would accept her mother's abusive ways.

"Momma, you're not going to help me get anything for school?" Ari asked.

"How many times I gotta tell yo' funky tail no! You think you grown, so go be grown! Where that lil boyfriend of yours? Get him to buy yo' stuff! I'm not helping you do nothin'," her mother spat.

"I barely ask you for anything. Why can't you help me? Aren't you happy I'm going to college? Everybody else I know has parents who support them. You've never supported me in anything, Momma; that's not fair!"

"Don't compare me to nobody's raggedy parents! You a piece of work, you know that? I don't know why you goin' to college anyway. You ain't gone never be nothin'! Just like yo daddy! You hear me! Nothin'! Like dried up gum under a chair! Get out my face!"

Ari frowned up. She wanted to throw a whole tantrum but she held it in. For the first time in her life, she allowed herself to say, "I hate you."

"Tramp, what did you just say?" Her mother asked before looking up at her.

Dissent made Ari wave her hand at her mother. She walked off and ran up the stairs. But her mother was on her heels. Before Ari could go into her bedroom, she snatched her by the hair, slapped her upside her face, and pulled her into the bathroom. She lifted up the toilet seat and pushed Ari's head into the bowl.

"You mop head little girl! I should kill you! You need to die!"

This beast spewed death as easy as it was for her to breathe. Did her mother hate herself and her life so much that she would allow herself to kill her own daughter?

The water from the bowl splashed all over the place, making it hard for Ari to hold on to its edges. She quickly reached up and flushed the toilet, catching her mother off guard. She then spun around and punched her mother in the face.

Ari didn't want to fight her mother, but she was so tired of this woman and the detestation that she continuously showed her. They scuffled for a few minutes until Ari slung her into her bedroom. She used that opportunity to run out of the house. This would be the last time she would be caught running out of this house. She wasn't coming back.

While fighting to catch her breath, Ari walked to the nearby gas station to get something to drink. Sirens sounded in the direction she was walking towards and the closer she got the more she could see. Two fire trucks, an ambulance, and a few police cars surrounded the area as well as yellow tape. Then she saw blood on the pavement. Her eyes bulged. *Who died?*

Ari saw a man lying on the pavement but couldn't see his face because of the crowd. Then she heard someone scream, "Noooooo! My baby! My baby! He was a good boy! My baby, Jesus no!"

The voice sounded recognizable. The chaos was too much to bear. Ari looked around in hopes of finding someone who had answers as to what happened to the man on the ground.

"Ari," another familiar voice called out to her.

She looked around and saw Evey with tears streaming down her face. Ari ran to Evey but Evey pushed her back, "Don't go over there you don't want to see this. Go back Ari! Go back!"

"What happened Evey? Who is that on the ground?"

67

Evey shook her head and looked Ari in the eyes, "Go back, Ari. You really don't want to see this."

Ari looked over Evey's shoulder and saw that it was Evey's mother crying. Her heart escaped her chest. It couldn't be who she thought it was.

"Evey, who is that on the ground?"

"It's Estavian. Somebody shot him."

Ari didn't believe Evey. She ran over to the scene and was able to see everything. It was Estavian lying on the ground. He was dead. He'd been shot in the chest. Ari wailed and collapsed to her knees. This could not be happening. Her life was shattering to pieces.

Come to find out, Estavian was caught in the wrong place at the wrong time. He walked into the middle of a robbery and accidentally scared the gunmen, who turned around and shot him out of fear. Estavian staggered out into the lot and died. As far as Ari knew it, her heart had died with him.

She walked away feeling like a zombie. Mrs. Akigbe talked to her about God and divine storms and told her that sometimes God allowed storms to happen to get people's attention. Nothing seemed divine about being abused by her mother, not knowing anything about her father, feeling like a misfit, and losing the love of her life. Who was she that God felt he needed her attention? And why did he have to do it this way?

Walking home was like torture. Instead of going inside, she walked around to the back of the house and sat on the back porch until the sun would no longer entertain her sorrows.

She'd calculated that her mother had probably gone to satisfy her gambling habit by now, and she'd calculated correctly. Walking inside the house was like walking into her soul both were empty and dark.

Ari walked upstairs to her room and into her closet. She pulled out a blank canvas and her art supplies. She sat the canvas on the easel and prepared her supplies to paint.

'There's purpose in your pain, Ari. Great pain comes before great purpose. Pay attention to the pain. It produces passion and passion pushes you straight into your purpose. For God so loved the world, he gave his only son up for the purpose of saving the same people who would take his life. Can your pain compare to this?" Mrs. Agibe directed her to this question the day that her artwork was trashed.

Ari wiped away her tears and immediately saw the image of Jesus on the cross. She put her brush to the canvas and painted what she saw.

QUEEN ARI
"… like medicine for her monsters …"

"My hopes and dreams are fading fast. I'm all burned out and I don't think my strength's going to last…"

If Ari would compare her life to anything right now it would be a lightbulb with a broken filament. Estavian was her filament. Her light source was snuffed out and lying in a casket. What kind of God allowed these types of tragedies to happen? Evey stood at the podium bellowing Yolanda Adams' "I Open Up My Heart," through her tears. Ari could feel Evey's pain from afar which forced her to hold hers in. *I'm not opening up my heart to a cruel God.*

Soft cries filled the room. The funeral was held at The Way, Truth, and Life Evangelical Church in Lansing, Illinois, a south suburban church where Estavian was baptized when he was a little boy. Ari wondered if anyone would miss him as much she did. She didn't feel like there was a reason to live.

She looked over at his mother who sat with a solemn expression on her face. Her face was damp from the many tears shed prior to walking into the church. Ari felt so much sorrow for her. Ari then felt a heavy dose of regret. How could she be so selfish? She lost her only son senselessly. *Of course she would miss him more than I would ever.* And somehow this woman would have to fight with all of her power to stay strong once she'd say her final goodbyes to him today.

"There is a time for everything and a season for every activity under the heavens. A time to be born and a time to die, a time to plant and a time to uproot."

"A time to kill and a time to heal, a time to weep and a time to dance, a time to scatter stones and a time to gather them, a time to embrace and a time to refrain from embracing, a time to search and a time to give up, a time to keep and a time to throw away, a time to tear and a time to mend, a time to be silent and a time to speak, a time to love and a time to hate, a time for war and a time for peace.

King Solomon the author of this scripture, Ecclesiastes 3:1-8 had an understanding of the different kinds of seasons we would face. A man of great wisdom and wealth knew happiness and sorrow. He knew what it meant to have and to see what he have, taken a way. He knew peace but he also knew war.

Believe it or not this life in God is an ongoing war. Yes, we will experience moments of peace, even moments of bliss, but I stand before you sons and daughters, to tell you that as long as we can bleed, we will be fighting. As long as the rhythm of our hearts beat in tandem with the plans that God thinks towards us, we are open to seasons of heartache. As long as we live on this planet Earth, we will see and experience things that will catch us off guard or throw us for a loop. We may not know all the ways of our Heavenly Father but we do know that God is sovereign and we do know that he's a comforter, so blessed are they that mourn! Those are the reassurances we can find in his word. He knew we would be treated unfairly from time to time and he knew that we would lose something to cause us to mourn. Did God not experience the same woes?"

"Why would he take my boy? Why would he take my friend? Why would He take someone like Estavian? He never hurt anybody! Normal questions and statements that are probably being shoved in your face right now by your own limited understanding. But can I ask you this question?

Why does a person have to hurt someone in order to receive the ultimate privilege of being present with God? Did you see what I just did? I shifted the perspective. We don't have a son who passed away on Earth. We have a king who lives in heaven with the Father. Do you see now? Fathom this, you might conclude that Jesus died an untimely and unfair death. But did he really? You say Estavian died an untimely and unfair death. But did he really? Estavian is reigning with his brother Jesus and present with the one and only true and living God! Yes! Yes! So dry your eyes my dear friends! This is the day the Lord has made! Let us rejoice and be glad in it!"

People stood up, clapped, and shouted praises including Estavian's mom. Ari stayed seated because she didn't know what was going on. She still couldn't figure out how to accept the pastor's explanation of what happened to her boyfriend. As far as she was concerned, this Heavenly Father he spoke of was a strange and selfish God. He owned all of heaven, all of Earth, and all of mankind but still took the only thing she called her own away from her.

Once the celebration of Estavian's death ended at the church, Ari rode in the limousine with his mother and Evey to the burial. The ride to the graveyard was quiet and quick.

Clouds formed in the late June sky and drizzle followed. Only a few of the people had an umbrella. Ari was a part of the group who didn't have one. As if she needed anymore rain in her life. Fortunately, a tent was set up at the burial site. Estavian's casket was placed into the ground by the pallbearers. Ari's stomach convulsed violently. She felt as if she would hurl. This was just too much to bear.

"Lord, we humbly stand before you surrounded by such a great cloud of witness. You know the language of our pain and you know the prayers that we don't utter. Today, we give this earthen vessel, Estavian Julian Niles, back to you Father. For we are sure, that neither death nor life, nor angels nor rulers, nor things present nor things to come, nor powers, nor height nor depth, nor anything else in creation, will be able to separate him from your love, God in Christ Jesus our Lord. Amen," the pastor prayed.

Everyone said Amen and then the casket slowly went into the ground. Some threw roses as the casket descended. Ari couldn't take it. She ran to where the limousine was parked. She covered her face as everything she'd been through over the course of every breath she'd taken until this point burst through her eyes. The light rain had long since stopped and the clouds begin to dissipate. The sun came out as if to say, "Hello." Ari immediately stopped crying. The warmth from the sun seemed to sooth her aching heart.

Then an eruption of butterflies calmed the seizure in her belly. This was the same feeling she would always experience whenever she would meet up with Estavian. She smirked a little.

"You ok Ari?" Evey asked with her hand on Ari's shoulder.

"I'm ok Evey. I'm ok," she replied.

A short while later, Estavian's mom walked up and embraced Ari. Her hug reverberated love and security something she never got from her own mother. After her fight with her mother, Ari, moved in with Estavian's family. She would stay there until school started in the fall where she would stay on campus.

"My Baby Doll. It's going to be just fine. Estavian is in a better place. You rest your pretty little heart. I know you loved him. But he would want you to rest your heart. He used the sun to smile back at you. You see?"

Ari wiped her eyes and smiled. What a comfort that was.

The three of them got into the limousine and was dropped off at home. Evey and Ari walked inside through the eerie silence. The two girls opted out of going to the repast. The temporary comfort Ari felt at the burial wouldn't be enough to make her socialize with people she didn't know. She was relieved Evey didn't want to go either.

Ari followed Evey upstairs to the bedroom but before they could make it all the way to the top of the stairs, Evey fell to her knees and wept. Ari sat down next to her on the stairs and held her friend. The two girls released their sadness for a few minutes. They then went to Evey's room to take a nap.

***

"Lift up your head oh ye' gates. I came that you might have life and that more abundantly. Take heart, I have overcome the world."

Ari heard a male's voice speak. She was sitting on a swing, swinging back and forward. She looked around all she could see was a lush green field and tall green trees standing beneath a crystal blue sky. She felt rays of what seemed like the sun shining on the right side of her face.

"Daddy is that you? Why won't you let me see your face? Can you take my heart? It's broken. I don't want it. I want a new heart. And I'm sad. I don't want to be sad anymore." Ari stated.

"Seek me and my strength. Seek my face continually. Until now you have not asked for anything in my name, ask and you will receive, so that your joy will be made full."

"What's your name? Oh please tell me your name! Father!"

"Seek and you will find."

Ari woke up abruptly. Evey was up packing. Ari sat up in the bed a little disoriented.

"Evey are you about to go somewhere? What's going on?"

Evey didn't respond. It was like she was in a trance or something. The room was like a library minus the occasional sniffs that came from Evey. Ari got out the bed and grabbed Evey's hand.

"Evey what's the matter?"

"I have to go, Ari. I can't stay here. I have to find myself. I can't stay here."

"Wait. What?" Ari asked in dismay.

They would both be starting college at the same place in a month. They would be roommates. She didn't understand why Evey was packing so early.

"I'm going to Atlanta. I want to stay with my granny. I don't want to stay here. Everything reminds me of Estavian. I don't want to remember him. I don't want to remember him!"

Evey went into the closet and begin to rip clothes off of hangers and throw them to the floor. Ari walked into the closet with her. She didn't know how to console her friend. *Why doesn't she want to remember him? Or maybe it is a good idea to forget.* Ari felt fire comb her heart at the thought of trying to forget Estavian.

"Ari, I'm sorry. I've made up my mind. I'm moving to Atlanta. I'm not going to go to school with you."

And just like that, the friendship that was like medicine for her monsters seemed to have come to an abrupt end.

QUEEN ARI

"She was no better than a dusty T.V. screen."

August

"So, there's no way I can get a dorm room to myself?"

"No, ma'am, only if you're an RA or a senior, but freshmen aren't allowed to have dorms by themselves at all."

Ari was irritable. She was unable to convince Evey to change her mind that night she told her she would not be accompanying her. Evey chose not to attend Columbia with Ari and moved to Atlanta with her mother for school instead. Ari would have followed Evey, but she really wanted to take advantage of the opportunity to study at Columbia (known for its great art and media programs). Either way, staying home with her mother was not an option. Since she'd had a taste of freedom staying as far away from her mother was something she'd made a law. But now she was stuck between a rock and a hard place. No friends, no family, and nobody to turn to except for a roommate she wasn't too eager to share her space with.

She walked into the dorm room to find one side of the small space was already taken. It really didn't matter to her though. Once becoming completely settled, she flopped onto the bed and laid there. She was still struggling with the death of Estavian. The pain was fresh and would resurface at the most inopportune times. Every minute of her life on up until now had molded her into a bitter cold girl. Tears seeped out of her eyes just as she heard the door opening. She quickly wiped her face and sat up.

"Oh, hey. Sorry, were you sleep?" The girl asked toting a crate in her arms and book bag on her back.

"No I wasn't," Ari said.

She watched as the girl put her crate and bookbag down, sat on her bed, and exhaled deeply.

"Woo, I'm so tired! I only had a few hours of sleep. Oh wow, how rude of me. My name is Mischa. Mischa Langston. And you are?"

"Ari Hughes."

"Nice to meet you, Honey Bunny!"

Ari thought Mischa's spirit was joyful enough, unlike her own. She really wanted to sleep away her misery instead of getting to know the girl though.

"So, did you check out anything yet? Oh my God, I can't believe I'm going to be living in downtown Chicago. What's a Southern belle like me supposed to do with herself in such a big city?" Mischa asked.

Ari chuckled. "You're from the South?"

"Not quite. I just lived down there for a while. I'm actually an army brat. I've lived some of everywhere. North Carolina just so happened to be the last stop before I came up here. I was actually born in Samoa. Now don't ask me what it was like. We left Samoa when I was four. I don't remember too much of anything. Where are you from?"

"I'm from Chicago-born and raised."

"I came up here with my mom and dad a few weeks ago just to sightsee. I love this city. I'm so excited that I live here now! Hey, can you show me around the dorms really quick?" Mischa excitedly asked.

Ari held in her sigh of reservation as she thought over her roommate's question. *What actually does she need to see?*

She shrugged her shoulders, slowly got out of her bed, slid into her flip flops, and motioned for Mischa to follow her. There really wasn't much to show and tell, as Ari was just as new to the campus as Mischa, so the tour ended as quickly as it started.

As the girls made it back to their living quarters, they were approached by a young man, wearing a red Girbaud hoodie and gray Nike gym shorts. He was tall and slim and his voice was deep and raspy.

"Y'all should come to our party," he said.

"What party?" Mischa asked.

"A back to school party on campus," he told her.

Ari wasn't in the mood for partying. She'd already reluctantly entertained Mischa by showing her around. She really just wanted to curl up under the covers and sleep the rest of the day away.

"We should! Ari you want to go? Please say yes. We can meet some more people. What do you think?"

"I don't feel like it. You can go without me," Ari responded.

"You not gone let yo' girl come to the party by herself are you? You don't have to stay till it ends. Just swing through for a minute. If anybody asks, tell them Red invited you, a'ight," he said before flashing a smile.

"Ok. Wait where will the party be?" Mischa inquired with eagerness.

"634 S. Wabash, across the street from Harold's," he told her and then walked away.

"He was cute, Ari, and he was staring at you."

"Whatever. I'm not interested. Why is he wearing a hoodie in August?"

***

Ari thought Mischa should have reconsidered choosing a major in Sports Medicine and go with Marketing. She was relentless with her pitch about this party that Ari had no ounce of interest in attending. Still, Mischa's constant badgering had worked.

She even did Ari's makeup and pressed her hair out, which was the main reason she relented.

"We look like sisters now, Ari," Mischa said after applying some gloss to her lips.

Ari continued to primp in the full-length mirror. She'd finally grown out of her boyish figure and the light blue Baby Phat jeans and fitted pink top she wore proved it.

As she brushed loose strands of hair off her shirt, she turned around and looked at Mischa. She was wearing the same brand of light blue jeans and fitted top that Ari had on, except hers was in white. Ari agreed that they did bear resemblance to each other. But the main give away was Mischa's 5'9 height and, according to magazine's standards, her plus size figure. All the things that made her plus sized, though, were well proportioned. She had wide hips and a derriere that went on for days. Mischa's breasts were so full that she could have easily blessed Ari with a cup or two, while still being the envy of the "itty bitty titty" committee. And to top it off, Mischa's confidence was off the charts.

Mischa's round reddish brown face glowed as she flicked her pressed out ebony tresses off her shoulders, and they rested comfortably at the center of her back, "You ready to party girl?"

The two girls headed to 634 S. Wabash- the address Red gave them. As it turns out, most of Columbia's math classes were held in this building and the party was on its lower level. The interior was colorful, modern, and had warehouse features. The area was filled with young adults some mingling, holding plastic red cups, and dancing to Twista's "Overnight Celebrity".

They hadn't been at the party all but ten minutes when Mischa was snatched away by a dark skinned guy with long dreads. His smile was engaging and handsome, but Ari still sensed something menacing about him. She figured it was just his tall stocky stature. Nevertheless, she allowed Mischa to be swept away by the midnight giant. She then resorted to her typical wallflower state. Crowds of this magnitude were not her thing, and she dared herself not to dance with anybody.

"Why you not dancing, Lil Mama?"

Ari stared blankly at the face of the only person she was somewhat accustomed to besides Mischa- the guy who invited them to the party, Red. She shrugged and then looked away. For some reason, she felt compelled to watch Mischa while she was with the guy neither one of them knew. Red handed her a cup, and she immediately sipped the fruity flavored concoction that was obviously mixed with alcohol.

"Where you from?" He asked.

"Here," She responded with no desire to elaborate and took a bigger sip.

"From the Chi?" He inquired.

"Yeah."

"I'm not from here. I'm from East St. Louis. My name Reginald but er'body call me Red," he told her, as he extended his right hand.

She shook it but kept her eyes on Mischa, who was now making out with this foreign man. Ari was appalled.

"Looks like yo girl havin' a good time," Red snickered.

Ari kept silent until he asked her name.

"It's Ari," she replied.

Some time had passed when one of 50 Cents fast paced songs faded out and made room for Joe's "More and More".

"Come on and dance with me," he invited.

Ari took her focus off of Mischa for a minute and gave Red her attention. She followed him to where everyone else was dancing. Allowing him to hold her from behind, she swayed to the rhythm of the song with her body pressed against his own. Her mind drifted away to a night she and Estavian slow danced inside of the loft that became known as their private getaway location. He was always so romantic and treated her better than anyone she ever knew. She missed him desperately. That alcohol began to quickly swallow her mind. She felt drowsy and her head felt like a balloon. She started to perspire.

Red wrapped his arms around Ari tighter and nibbled on her neck. She imagined Estavian holding her close to him and soaking in her sweet perfume. She could smell the Curve cologne he used to wear faithfully. Her eyes swelled with tears when she heard,

"I miss you, Ari."

"Huh?"

"I said, I like you, Ari," Red said.

And just like that Estavian was gone. She turned around and looked in Red's face. While searching for her deceased lover's face, she realized that Red was actually more handsome than she thought.

He reminded her of the R&B artist Tank, with those signature smiling eyes. She was angry with herself for being carried away by her thoughts. She looked away to where Mischa was still dancing with the giant. She'd actually focused her attention on them just in time to see him put something in a cup and give it to Mischa.

Ari rushed over to Mischa, although all her movements seemed to be in slow motion. She smacked the cup out of Mischa's hands.

"Hey! Why did you do that, Ari?"

"He put something in your drink! I knew it was something about him I didn't like. Let's go back to the dorms."

"Man you trippin'," he yelled back at Ari obviously upset that she'd busted him out.

"Ari I think you had too much to drink. Maybe you should just go back," Mischa said.

Ari squinted in confusion. What did she mean, too much to drink? She'd only had one cup, but she did feel unlike herself. By now, she was burning up and her eyes were heavy like she'd taken some cough syrup.

"I'm not going back to the dorms by myself!"

"I'll walk with you," Red said.

Ari glared at Red. He shouldn't have been the one volunteering to walk back to the dorms with her. She automatically figured that she and Mischa should have been leaving together since "together" is how they came.

She was pissed but in no mood to argue. *What did I expect of a girl that I just met today anyway? This wasn't Evey. Evey would have never left me hanging like that. Then again, who knows what Evey would have done? After all, she did leave me here in Chicago by myself.*

"Come on, Ari. It's good. I can walk you back."

Ari let out a huge exhale that encompassed all of her frustrations. Mischa wasn't even receptive. This stranger may not have had the chance to get her to drink whatever it was he put in that cup, but she was clearly drugged with infatuation nevertheless. Ari reluctantly walked away with Red, even though he was practically a stranger too. She felt like everyone was a stranger and everyone sucked. As a matter of fact, she felt that her *whole life* sucked. She shoved the door open and stormed out the building.

"Damn, slow down Lil Mama," she heard Red from behind.

She wasn't going to slow down, since now her bladder was full. The August night sky was clear and the moon was full. The light breeze was pleasant on her sticky skin.

"Hey, Baby why you walking so fast?"

"I gotta pee!"

Red didn't say anything else but continued to trail her. They made it to her dorm room when Ari suddenly remembered her entire wallet with her key card to get into the room was in Mischa's purse.

"Dammit!"

"What's wrong, Baby?"

She didn't know what caused more fury, the fact she didn't have her key card or the fact that he kept calling her Baby. She huffed, "I don't have my key card."

"Aw man, yo. Well come to my room then."

Ari looked at him with a turned up face, "No!"

"Don'tchu gotta pee?"

She felt trapped. "Alright. Where's your room?"

He said nothing and took her by the hand. She wasn't going to admit it but she needed his hand because she was feeling drowsier by the minute. *Why the heck am I feeling like this?*

It seemed as if they were walking forever. Maybe it had something to do with her not being completely present mentally. But as they finally approached his residence, she realized he actually lived in the student apartments off campus. He lied, but she wasn't in the right frame of mind to confront him on it. He opened up the door and showed her to the bathroom.

And what a relief it was to release all that she'd been holding since leaving the party. After being completely drained, she wiped herself, flushed the toilet, and pulled up her clothes. She went to the sink and washed her hands before splashing her face with cold water to get rid of the woozy feeling. She'd never had alcohol before, so she wasn't sure if this response was typical. Needless to say, she hated not being completely in control of her body.

Knock! Knock!

"You a'ight in there, Baby?"

Ari rolled her eyes and quickly opened the door, "Why do you keep calling me Baby? I'm not your baby!"

"Well, damn ma! That's how you feel?"

She retreated a little. She didn't know how she felt. Honestly she just wanted to lie down for a minute.

"Where can I sleep? I want to go to bed."

85

"That's cool. Come on to my room," he guided.

Then she felt apprehensive. She was not about to go in his room. *Why did I come to his place? Am I stupid or something?* She didn't know him from Adam. But now she had no choice.

She was obviously under the influence and she was sure he was not going to walk her back to the dorms now. This most certainly felt like a set up.

"A'ight you can sleep on the couch then," he said before going into his room to bring out a blanket and pillow.

He handed the pillow and blanket to her, "Here."

She took them and walked to the couch and folded the blanket in half placing the pillow on top of it. Red walked away and went into to his room then closed the door. Once taking off her shoes she flopped down on the couch. It wasn't as comfortable as a bed but it would make do for the night. She fell asleep a few minutes later.

Her sleep was broken due to a dream she had about Estavian. He always invaded her dreams. This one however was different. It was a dream of them making love. It was vivid enough that her entire body was drenched in sweat. Once awake, she pulled off her jeans and placed her hands on her treasure chest as the warmth percolated through her panties like heat from a vent. This had never ever happened to her before-being aroused by a dream that is.

She got up from the couch, crept to Red's bedroom door and softly knocked on it. No answer. She turned the knob and, to her surprise, the door opened with ease. Red was lying in bed on his stomach with his eyes closed. Ari wanted to take advantage of him, though she had never done anything remotely similar to that before. She crept over to the bed and climbed in on the other side of Red.

He woke up, somewhat alarmed, and turned his head around to her, "What you doing Ba---I mean Ari."

"I had a bad dream," she fibbed. He lied about taking her to a dorm, so did it matter that she lied too?

"Aw, ok," he said then positioned himself on his side with his back to her.

She was upset. She wanted him to take the bait. Why didn't he? She scooted closer to him and rubbed her hand down his spine. He jerked but didn't say a word. She kissed his naked shoulder blade and he jerked again but turned around to face her.

"Ari, whatchu doing?"

"I thought you said you liked me?"

"I, I do but you…"

Before he could say anything else she climbed on top of him and started kissing him. Still somewhat in shock, Red kept his hands free until Ari grinded against him. She stopped momentarily to take off the rest of her clothes and to allow him to take off his boxers and put on a condom. She attacked him with her kisses again and reenacted the dream she had. For a minute she felt as if she were being unfaithful. But then again, how could she be unfaithful to someone who was dead?

***

The next morning Ari awoke to the smell of bacon. She got up and put on her shirt and panties, then sauntered into the kitchen. Shirtless, Red had prepared pancakes, bacon, and eggs for breakfast.

He turned around while smiling when she walked in, "Hey Baby, I made you breakfast."

She stood there for a moment. She didn't want breakfast. She wanted to go to her dorm and take a shower.

"Sit down so you can eat."

She hesitated and sat down. He'd done a good job with this breakfast. Nothing was burnt or half done. He even had orange juice. She looked at him blankly.

"What? Don't tell me you don't eat pork."

"I do."

Before they could eat, he took her hands. She had no clue what he was about to do.

"Close your eyes and bow your head for grace."

As he closed his eyes and bowed his head, she scrunched up her face and thought silently, *"For grace?"*

"Thank you God for today. Thank you for the food that we 'bout to receive, and bless those who are not fortunate enough to eat. Amen."

"Amen."

Ari had never said grace before eating. She was completely caught off guard. Honestly, she had always thought that was something people only did on T.V. She ate her breakfast but could barely enjoy it because Red would not stop staring at her.

"Are you going to look at me the entire time I eat or what?"

"I'm sorry. I can't help it. I just think you're beautiful, that's all."

"Oh, thank you."

He started chuckling a little.

Somewhat annoyed Ari glared at him, "What's funny?"

"Nothing. You really surprised me last night. I wasn't expecting you to do that."

"Do what?"

"You know, make the first move. I always thought girls didn't do that."

Ari was offended, "What are you trying to say?"

"Nothing, I'm not saying it in a bad way. It probably was the Ecstasy you had,"

Ari looked at him boggled. He gave her the impression that he should have kept that last part to himself. He diverted his eyes from her direction, as if an extra amount of attention needed to be given to his plate of food all of a sudden. She replayed the events of the night before in her mind, as her heart raced. She'd only had the drink that he'd given her, and she remembered feeling weird shortly after drinking it!

Her eyes burned a hole in his face, as she shouted her next question, "You drugged me?"

Red looked back at her cowardly, "Naw. Actually Prentice, he—,"

"Who the hell is Prentice?" Ari cut him off.

"Prentice is the tall dude wit' the dreads that was wit' yo' girlfriend. I had got me something to drink and he put it in there. He told me to give it to a girl so it could take the edge off her or something."

"So you gave it to me to take advantage of me! You listened to that loser and drugged me. I should tell the campus police on you and your perverted friend! You know you can go to jail, right? What if I'd reacted badly to this drug? What did you say it was again- Ecstasy? Yeah, I should tell!"

Ari was furious and Red's pitiful puppy dog face wasn't going to diffuse her temper. She figured she was actually dumb for allowing herself to get to this point anyway.

Slamming her hands on the table, she got up from her seat. Her chair fell to the ground with a loud crash, and Red followed her every move with his eyes.

"Where you going? Ari, you ain't gone tell on me are you? I could get kicked out of school."

"I don't give a damn! You took advantage of me!"

Ari searched for her belongings. She needed to get out of there and take a shower. She quickly put on her jeans and socks after finding them balled up under the covers on the couch.

"Well to be honest, Ari, you took advantage of me. I didn't bother you. You came into my room. I didn't make you do that."

"You---," She stopped herself. He was right. There was no arguing with him anymore. What would she tell the campus police? They would laugh at her story. She flopped down on the couch, as various emotions ran their race through her psyche.

"Ari, I'm sorry. I, I hope this doesn't make you look at me as some kind of predator or nothing. As a matter of fact, I need to tell you a secret."

Ari never really acknowledged Red. Instead, she stared at the T.V. screen with a disgusted look on her face. The screen needed to be dusted off. She compared herself to it. She was no better than a dusty T.V. screen. Her life needed to be dusted off too.

"Did you hear me, Ari? I said I got a secret I need to tell you."

Red's voice was annoying and interfering with her attempts to bury herself in regret, "What is it, Red? What's your secret?"

"Well, before last night with you, I was… I was a virgin."

She snapped out of it and turned in his direction. His face was a combination of embarrassment and sincerity. She shook her head. The campus police would most definitely laugh at her.

QUEEN ARI
"And he had stolen space in her land of la la…"

February 2005

Ari briskly walked down the streets of downtown on her way to work. She'd managed to snag a part time job at Starbucks over the summer to help pay for the things she needed. Her job also afforded her the ability to get a cellphone- something that almost all the students on campus had.

The salt on the ground crunched underneath her brown UGG boots. She was trying her best not to miss a beat because she hated being late for anything. Unfortunately, it was looking like her track record of timeliness was going to be blemished today. She was but a few feet away from her job when her phone vibrated in her coat pocket. Cold air huffed out of her mouth as she exhaled and pulled the agitated phone out

Flipping it open with her chin, she answered, "Hello?"

"Hey Baby. You at work yet? I was just tryin' to catch you before you clocked in."

It was Red. She found herself tangled up in a relationship with him not too long after that infamous night this past summer. It was a relationship based on nothing but convenience. She had nowhere to go during the winter break from school, so she stayed with him.

Ari allowed Red to believe that she was in this thing just as a much as he was, even though that couldn't have been further from the truth.

She had just invested too much into their situation to pull out of it. At least that was going to be the case until she either graduated or could afford to live on her own.

"I'm actually not too far from work now. What's the matter?"

"I just was callin' to see if you wanted to go out tonight."

"It's Wednesday, Red. You know I don't like going out on weekdays. And I got a quiz to study for anyway."

"But Baby, I haven't seen you since Sunday. I wanna see you today, just for a little bit. Maybe I can come up to your job for lunch."

Ari exhaled again. Red was really a sweet guy. She didn't deserve him. She was no good for him or anybody else for that matter right now. Nevertheless, she would not let him come up to her job. She preferred to keep a strict line between work and her personal life. Plus her coworkers were super nosey.

"No Red. I will just meet you at your place when I get off work tonight."

"Well what if I meet you at your job when you get off?"

Ari's face crumpled up. *Why does he insist on coming to my job?*

"Red I told---,"

Before she could finish her sentence, she slipped on some black ice right in front of the door to Starbucks. Her phone flew out of her hand and slid a few feet away. To say that she was embarrassed was a gross understatement.

"Here; take my hand, Sweetheart."

She looked up to see a man with his hand extended down to her. She took his hand as she pulled herself up.

"You ok, Baby girl?" The man asked.

93

"Yeah," she responded, walking over to pick up her cellphone. Unlike her ego, it wasn't damaged. She looked at the screen to see that Red was still on the line calling her name.

"Are you sure you didn't bump your head or anything? Concussions are no joke."

"No, I'm fine. Really, I am. Thank you," she reassured him with a slight attitude. After a few glances, she realized he was really nice looking with his dark brown skin and friendly smile. She walked past him and rushed toward the revolving doors of Starbucks. To her horror, he followed her inside. She briskly walked to the back, where the employee closet was located.

"Hey, Ari, are you okay? They told me you fell outside by the door."

"Yeah, I'm fine, Ms. Lisa. Thanks,"

"You seem a little shaken up. I'm going to make a hot cocoa for you, just the way you like it."

Ms. Lisa smiled at Ari with her usual expression of happiness. Ms. Lisa was Ari's supervisor and always treated her with kindness. She patted Ari on the shoulder and walked away. Her departure gave Ari time to collect her nerves and reconfigure her scrambled thoughts.

A short while later, Ms. Lisa came back carrying a small cup of hot cocoa with hazelnut and handed it to Ari. She stood there as her pale skin flushed pink and tugged on her strawberry blond French braid that was sitting on her right shoulder. Her blue eyes shifted back and forth, which gave Ari the impression that she had something to say to her.

"Ms. Lisa, is everything ok?"

"Oh, yeah; it is. Well, there's a very nice gentleman out in the lobby looking for you. I was just wondering if you would like for me to tell him you'd be out shortly."

Considering her shift started about a good fifteen minutes ago, she had no choice but to go see who this "nice gentleman" was.

After taking a few sips of the hot cocoa Ms. Lisa made for her, she walked to the register she would be working from for her shift. She looked around where the customers were and didn't see anybody looking as if they were waiting for her. Then over to her right side she saw that someone wearing a familiar black, military style coat and a red baseball cap rising from his seat. She closed her eyes and shook her head. It was Red.

He turned around and threw a Starbucks cup into the trashcan. As Ari expected, he came directly toward her. She thought he must have been close by her job during their phone conversation because he flew there.

"That's the guy that asked for you Ari. Do you know him?" one of her coworkers asked.

"Yeah," she spoke through clinched teeth.

"Hey, Baby," Red spoke, obviously eager to see her.

Ari quickly walked around the counter and stood on the same side he was on. She grabbed his arm and pulled him closer to the entrance of Starbucks. It really didn't matter how far they went though; prying eyes followed their every move. Despite the cold temperature, she forced him outside with her in an attempt to have some privacy. She tried her hardest to contain her displeasure. Red didn't mean any harm, but she couldn't help feeling disrespected.

"I thought I told you not to come up here!"

"I wasn't gone come, but I was worried 'bout you. It sounded like yo' phone had been knocked out of yo' hands or somethin'. I didn't know what to think. I was scared. I'm sorry."

Ari smacked her lips. She probably would have done the same thing. She looked up at his innocent face. Everything about him was right except for his decision to love her. She wanted to give him a hug to reassure him that she wasn't upset with him caring but too many eyes were focused in their direction.

"I will see you when I get off okay? We can hang out," she told him.

His face lit up, "Really? Even though it's Wednesday?"

"Yeah, Babe. Even though it's Wednesday."

***

Gratefully, Ari's shift at Starbucks went by quickly. No complaints or drawer shortages. She'd almost forgotten her promise to go to Red's after work until her coworker Sherry called out to her,

"So who was that cute fella that came up here for you? Is that your boyfriend?"

She knew somebody would ask. As she put on her BabyPhat coat and bundled up, she answered Sherry unenthusiastically, "Yeah, that's my boyfriend."

"Ooooh wee, he is too fine. Y'all go to school together?"

"Yup."

"Aw ok. Do he have any friends?" Sherry asked.

"Um, I don't know. I got to run and meet him somewhere. Goodnight, Girl," Ari quickly told her before rushing out of there. There was no need to hang around and gossip with Sherry about her personal life. She'd already told her too much anyway.

"Hey, Lady," a male voice spoke behind her from a distance.

Ari turned around in search of the person who had spoken. It wasn't Red; she knew that much. It was dark out, and she really didn't want to take the place of a curious cat so she kept walking.

She heard crunching of salt increase, meaning that the man was quickening his steps behind her. Ari grabbed onto the pepper spray Mischa bought her a few months ago after they heard about two girls being attacked on campus before winter break. She abruptly stopped in her tracks and turned around with her finger resting upon the push-button of the container.

"Back up before I spray you! Don't come any further," she screamed.

"Heeeeyy! Ok, ok," the guy said, with his hands raised in surrender.

"Oh, what do you want?" She asked him.

After further inspection, she quickly realized he was the guy who helped her up from her fall earlier. It didn't matter though. It was night and common faces blended in with the unfamiliar ones. She stood still, with her gloved finger ready to spray him with peppered fire. Her coworkers rushed out of the Starbucks and looked at the two of them.

"You ok, Ari?" Ms. Lisa asked.

Ari spoke before she thought, "Yeah, I'm ok, Ms. Lisa."

She gave the man her attention again, "What do you want?"

"I didn't mean to frighten you or make you feel uncomfortable. I just came back here because I was a little concerned about you after that fall you had. I wanted to see if you were ok."

His hands were still raised, and it was clear that he was being upfront. Ari didn't want to register what he'd said though. A perfect stranger was concerned about her? Really? She didn't know how to respond to that. As she looked behind him to see her coworkers walking away in the distance, she debated on what to say next.

"I'm...I told you I was fine earlier when you helped me up. I'm ok."

His smile could have blinded her. He straightened his paperboy hat and held out his hand covered with a leather glove, "Thaddeus."

She slowly put away her liquid weapon and gave him a few inches of her space to take his hand. His cologne thrashed the cold air. Ari didn't feel threatened anymore. His grip was magnetic, and she was trapped in its pull.

"My name's Ari. Nice to meet you, Thaddeus."

His eyes that stared at her so intently made her warm. It felt too good. She cleared her throat to break the small silence, and suddenly remembered that she was supposed to be heading to Red's, "I...I have to...to go. I have someplace to be."

"That's fine, I'm just glad you're alright. Here, take my card. Call me any time," he told her, before taking a business card out of a silver cardholder.

She took the card but didn't know what she'd really use it for, "Thanks. Have a good night."

"You too, Ari. Be safe and watch out for that black ice."

Ari chuckled and walked towards Michigan Avenue, inwardly wishing she'd never told Red she would come over his house tonight. Mr. Thaddeus was an uninvited guest. And he'd stolen space in her land of la la. But she wasn't sure if she wanted to evict him.

QUEEN ARI
"... sounds of the shower..."

March

"I can't wait until I stop having periods. I hate Eve," Mischa said rubbing her abdomen.

Ari shook her head while she sat at the study in their dorm room. Classes ended today for spring break. As usual, Mischa would be going back to Charlotte and she, of course, was headed back to Red's.

Mischa crouched down and pulled a clear container from under her bed, frantically searching for something.

"What are you looking for?"

"My box of tampons. I thought I had at a least few in here."

"If you can't find them, you can have some of mine."

Ari got up and went into the closet. She dragged a medium sized tote out with her. After removing its top, she told Mischa to help herself to whatever she needed. Mischa discovered that the bin was filled with a host of sanitary items and smirked.

"Girl, you got a baby Walgreens up in here," Mischa laughed.

Ari sat down back at the study. It was better to have a lot of what she needed as oppose to nothing at all. Her struggles during her adolescent years taught her that. Her phone notified her that she'd received a text message. She reached for her phone and read the message.

"Happy Friday, Ari."

Ari flashed a smile.

"Who just made you gush like crazy, Ari? Is it Red?"

"No. Thaddeus."

Mischa gasped, "Wait who the heck is Thaddeus? You're cheating on Red?"

"No! Thaddeus is just my friend. I met him at my job."

"Your friend? Why am I just now hearing about, Thaddeus? Oh my God tell me about this friend."

Ari giggled, "There's nothing really to tell you. I met him last month when I fell in front of my job. You remember? I told you that's why my phone acts up sometimes. Well he came back that night claiming he was worried about me. He gave me his card, but I never used it. Then the man started coming up to my job asking me when I was going to call him. So, one day I texted him, but I didn't really expect him to respond. I was kind of hoping he didn't because he's an older guy."

Mischa gasped, "How much older? Is he a grandpa?"

"Ew! No! He's in his early thirties," Ari told her.

"Aw ok. Well that's not that bad. So, what happened next? He responded, and now he's been texting you ever since then? I was wondering who were you texting late at night. I never knew you and Red to be texters like that. Hmmm. I take it you like him?"

"I do! It's so weird. I only get to see him when I'm at work, and then we text when I get off. I don't think I've ever felt this way about anyone. Well, not since my first love, Estavian."

"Oh yeah, the one that passed away."

The mention of Estavian and his unfortunate death tinged her heart. She still had Mischa's undivided attention, but there was nothing else to tell her.

She actually wished she did have more to share. She quickly changed the subject, "We should go to the movies tonight with Red and Prentice since you're leaving tomorrow.

"You know what? That sounds like a good idea, Girl. I'm going to see if Prentice wants to do that," Mischa responded.

Ari kicked herself in the butt for that idea. She hadn't really been a fan of Prentice since the night that Red told her Prentice encouraged him to drug a girl at the back to school campus party. To make matters worse, that girl wound up being her. Ari wondered why Mischa never picked up on his shadiness. Maybe it had something to do with her not being too street smart.

She halfheartedly responded, "You know what on second thought, I'll let you know." Later on that afternoon, after packing up the rest of her belongings, she called Red once again. She'd actually been trying to contact him all day because he would be the one to come help her move her belongings to his place. For some reason, though, he wasn't responding to any of her texts or calls. She was more angry than worried.

"When's the last time you heard from him, Ari?" Mischa asked, with a worried look on her face.

It was looking like the idea of going on a double date would be cancelled, so the two of them grabbed something to eat from Subway. The sun was setting, and the gusty spring winds wrestled with both their hair as they walked back to their dorm.

"When I got off work yesterday afternoon. He told me he was off today, so he would be able to help me bring my things to his place. I don't understand what could have happened between yesterday and now. He knows I don't like it when he doesn't communicate stuff to me. If something came up, just tell me so I can know what I need to do. I hate feeling helpless," Ari said.

"Well, if he doesn't call you while we're eating our food, do you want me to take you over there to see if he's home?"

Bingo! This was the perfect invitation to be a stalker. Not that Ari wanted to give herself that title, but she really wanted to know why Red was suddenly tarnishing his track record of being consistent with her. Especially when he knew she needed him the most right now. As she and Evey would say, Mischa hadn't said nothing but a word.

Red hadn't called or texted her while they ate, and Ari was too anxious to really even enjoy her food. Something just wasn't right. She wrapped up her food and put it to the side, "Mischa let's just go now."

Mischa sucked juice through the straw of her drink then placed it on the study before grabbing her purse and her car keys. The ride to Red's was not long, but it was now dark. Ari wished she had told Mischa to stay in the car but it was too late; Mischa hopped out the car as fast as she did. Unbeknownst to Red, Ari had secretly gone and got a key made to his apartment. She never used it until now.

Both Ari and Mischa walked into the apartment complex and took the stairs up to the second floor. Once arriving at the door, Ari pressed her ear up against it and heard a radio playing.

She bit her bottom lip because she assumed Red had to be home. She put the key in the doorknob, slowly opened the door, and walked inside with Mischa following closely behind her.

To her surprise, no one was in the living area but Usher's "Confessions II" was playing on the radio. Her attention was immediately directed towards the bathroom, where she heard the sounds of the shower running.

"Mischa, stay in here," she whispered.

Ari tiptoed to the bathroom and heard Red's voice, as well as that of a woman. Her left eyebrow rose as she continued to listen to what sounded like them kissing. Rage and jealousy ignited in the pit of her stomach. She took two steps back and walked past Mischa and headed into the kitchen. Mischa followed her.

"What are you about to do, Ari? Where's Red?"

Ari turned on the hot water in the sink and filled up a pot. She briskly walked with the pot into the bathroom. She lifted up the pot and threw the water over the shower curtain. Red and the girl hollered out loud. He cursed and pulled back the shower curtain, where he immediately was greeted by Ari's wrath. She leaned in and began to shoot fists of fury, wildly punching Red's naked wet body. Mischa rushed into the bathroom and pulled Ari out. The two girls waited in the living room for him and his "new thing" to come out of the bathroom. Ari could hear him telling the girl to go into the room. It was best she did obey or she would risk being pummeled if she tried to intervene.

"Ari, what the heck is wrong with you? Are you crazy?"

"Excuse me? What do you mean 'what's wrong with me?' What's wrong with you, Red? You had me sitting in the dorms waiting on your butt to come pick me up. All the while you're here taking a shower with that heffa!"

"You must didn't read my text when I told you it was over. Stop pretending like you want to be with me now that you ain't got no place to go. I don't know what you came over here for. But since you here, you can get the stuff you left here and go," Red said, as he walked over to the door where a black garbage bag was sitting.

Ari stood bewildered, angry, and humiliated. *He sent me a text? When? And who breaks up with someone through text?* She wanted to rip him a new one but that would have been a lost cause. How Red felt was justified. How he handled it, though, was unjustified. Ari walked toward the door and snatched the garbage bag out of Red's hands before leaving his apartment. Mischa followed her without talking.

Back to the dorms, bombarded by a mixture of emotions, Ari couldn't fight the unrelenting question, "Where am I going to go now?"

As if Mischa heard the question, she broke up Ari's anxiety, "You can always come home with me to Charlotte. My parents wouldn't mind."

That sounded like a good idea. But Ari felt as if she wasn't good at depending on people. Never could depend on her mother. Never could depend on her father. Never could depend on anyone for that matter. *If I decline this offer, where would I go?* A shelter seemed like her only other option.

As Mischa pulled the car into the lot designated for students, Ari's phone buzzed in her pocket. She pulled it out, slightly hoping it was Red. He always seemed to rescue her from her own indecisiveness.

"Hello, Ari," the text read.

It was Thaddeus. She debated responding before flipping the phone back shut. After taking her belongings out of the car, she made the walk of shame to the dorms. She was glad Mischa didn't bother her with any more comments or questions. She wasn't in the mood to talk. Too bad Thaddeus wasn't around to get the memo.

"I want to see you," he texted.

"So what are you going to do, Ari? Do you want to come to Charlotte with me?" Mischa asked.

Ari took a deep breath, "No. No, that's ok. I have someplace to go."

QUEEN ARI

"The liquid tasted like pineapples and poison..."

"You can stay here as long as you need to," Thaddeus told Ari.

Ari with just a small level of reservation told him her current situation which was partly humiliating yet refreshing once he rushed to her aide like a knight in shining armor. He brought all of her belongings to his condo in the South Loop of Chicago. She had never been to his place before, so she was excited to see how he lived. Ari dropped her book bag on the floor and walked towards the living area.

"Wait, Baby; take your shoes off, "he said.

"Oh, I'm sorry," she said, as she took off her white K-Swiss.

"Are you hungry?"

"No."

"Ok. Well, I'll be back."

Ari sat down on the midnight blue suede couch that felt like heaven to her bottom. Despite the comfort of the sofa, she couldn't relax too much. She was actually very antsy. She barely knew this man and now she was in his home. This was the place she'd agreed to stay since she had no living arrangements besides Mischa's.

Puddles of sweat formed in the palm of her hands. Without any additional deliberation, Ari popped up from her seat and ran to the door to put on her shoes before Thaddeus came back. How naïve was she to accept this man's offer to stay with him? Thanks to her bad timing, he caught her putting on her shoes and rushed to stop her.

"What are you doing, Ari?" He asked, while gently sliding the shoes from her now trembling hands.

His voice was calm and medicinal. Betrayed by her emotions, tears formed in her eyes and poured down her cheeks. She held her head down and sobbed.

"Ari, I know you're scared. It's ok. I want to help you and I want to protect you. I'm not a bad guy. If you want you can give all my information to one of your friends. But you don't have to be afraid of me. I don't want to hurt you. You're too precious to me," He comforted, as he pulled her into his chest. He kissed her on the forehead and lightly brushed his hand against her back until she was calmed.

He took her by the hand and sat her down, back onto the couch. He handed her a dark blue chalice and told her to drink what was inside. She was skeptical at first and took a huge gulp. Thaddeus laughed out loud, "You're going to regret that later."

Ari looked at him confused. Hadn't she got enough of drinking alien beverages? The liquid tasted like pineapples and poison. Her chest burned fiercely.

"Take another small sip. It will stop your chest from burning."

"What's in here?"

"Vodka."

She vacuumed the air with her gasp. She told herself she would never drink alcohol again, yet here she was guzzling this concoction like Kool-aid. And after drinking a third cup that was less potent, life just seemed to be a figment of her imagination. She flopped back onto the sofa that now felt like a bed of clouds and exhaled.

Thaddeus sat at the opposite end of the couch with his head resting on the back of it. His eyes were closed and Ari assumed that he was probably gallivanting in his thoughts. She sat up and looked at him closer. She began to admire how perfectly sculpted his face was. She noticed how his thick beard and mustache accentuated his strong structured cheekbones and jawline. His dark face was perfectly smooth, minus the small birthmark near his eye. His rugged attractiveness aroused her.

With a drunken impulse, she straddled him and kissed his lips. Thaddeus opened his eyes, "What are you doing, Ari?"

She didn't answer him. Instead she attempted to kiss him again, expecting him to kiss her back but he didn't.

"Stop it, Ari. Get off me," he said sternly.

She leaned to kiss his neck, but he grabbed her by the waist and roughly sat her back onto the couch. He got up and grabbed his keys from off the table and left out of the house leaving Ari there on the bed of clouds.

***

Ari awoke the next day feeling like she'd been beaten with a sledgehammer. Her head throbbed terribly. She smelled something cooking. The aroma was pleasing for a few seconds but then it triggered nausea. She ran straight into the bathroom and hurled everything but her social security number into the toilet. Completely detoxified, she rested her head on the cold seat of the toilet. Footsteps prompted her to flush the toilet and wash her face with cold water.

Thaddeus came into the bathroom with a cup of orange juice. "Here. Take this and drink it down with the orange juice."

"No. I don't want it," she rudely declined.

"You have a hangover, Sweetie. This will help you. It's not alcohol."

"Hardhead makes a soft a--," her mother would often say.

In this case, a hardhead made a sour stomach. "That's what I get", she thought as she took the pill and swallowed it down with the orange juice. Ari handed him the cup, and he helped her off the floor.

"You need to put something back into your stomach."

"I don't have an appetite right now."

"You don't have to eat an entire meal but you need to eat something."

Ari followed Thaddeus into the kitchen where two plates of breakfast sat at the island. He pulled the bar stool out for her to take a seat. He'd prepared toast, turkey sausages, and cheese omelets. She felt as if his eyes were like mini surveillance cameras as she picked at the food. She really didn't want any of it.

"You don't have any manners," he said casually.

She looked at him somewhat offended.

"How is it in one moment, you were going to run out of my house without saying a word? Then the next moment you try to seduce me? You have no manners or tact. It's ok though. I can tell you haven't been trained properly. I can train you."

Ari turned up her lips, "Trained? I'm not a puppy you found on the street. You don't have to housebreak me. I *do* have manners!"

Thaddeus stared at her blankly for a minute then continued to eat. This man was working her nerves already. He wasn't easy to manipulate or run over like Red, that is until yesterday.

Come to think about it, the only man she knew for a while other than Estavian, was Lonzo with his false sense of authority and toxic methods of control, she utterly despised. That abhorrence for him and resentment and hidden anger towards her absent father did not discriminate either. They'd just married her personality, giving birth to her bad attitude. Maybe he was right. Maybe she *did* need to be trained.

QUEEN ARI
"Who have I become?"

September

"So he still hasn't touched you?" Mischa asked while slurping a smoothie out of her cup. It was a sunny Friday afternoon, and the girls were both done with classes for the day. Ari didn't have to work either. She'd managed to get the weekend off to celebrate her 19th birthday that was coming up this Tuesday. They decided to hang out at one of their favorite spots- Jamba Juice on State and Randolph.

"No! I don't know what the problem is. Nothing that I try to do to entice him works. Maybe he doesn't like girls. That has to be it. How do you sleep in the same bed with a girl and never want to touch her?"

"Maybe so, but he doesn't strike me as the gay type, you know? Like Kentrell?"

"Aw yeah, you're right about that."

The girls shook their heads in unison. "It could be a good thing though. He may just be the gentleman you need. There aren't a lot of gentlemen out here, Ari. Plus, guys tend to change after you give them some. I don't know why that is though," Mischa seemed to drift off into her own thoughts.

Ari sat there quietly and allowed her thoughts to converse with one another. *Could he be the type of gentleman I used to daydream about during my virgin days? What if he really is the man that I thought I'd marry before I gave myself to Estavian? Now look at me. I'm actually sitting here questioning his sexuality because he doesn't want to sleep with me!*

Who have I become? If her mother knew she was sleeping around, she would have stomped a mud hole into her back. Her mother may have had some cruel ways, but she didn't play when it came to Ari giving her body way. She would always say, "Premarital sex breeds premarital problems." That's because she conceived Ari out of wedlock and didn't want her daughter to make the same mistake.

Well, it was too late for that. Ari was no longer a virgin. She'd tasted the forbidden fruit her mother warned her about so many times, and now she was as horny as a dog in heat. She wanted to be touched.

Later on that night, Ari and Mischa went to a party off campus. Everybody who knew somebody was there. Ari had firmly made up in her mind that she would not be drinking anything in a red plastic cup, a Styrofoam cup, or any cup for that matter. She wanted to just have fun without any influence from alcohol. The crowd was growing larger by the hour. There was dancing, small talking, and rap battling buzzing throughout the room. The atmosphere was live, and Ari was soaking it all up. She was young with no immediate worries and for a minute she felt free. Ari swayed to "Like You", by Bow Wow and Ciara from her seat on a window seal.

Her eyes were closed as she mouthed the words to the song. When she finally opened them, a guy was walking directly toward her. He wore a tapered curly fro that was as black as a raven. His face was dark brown and he had deep dark eyes. He smiled at her with perfect pearly white teeth.

Although she was living with an older man and basically being taken care of by him, he barely showed her any attention. So, she guilelessly flirted with whoever noticed her. By this point, she'd broken out of her insecure shell and wanted to be seen. She was feeling herself.

He boldly positioned himself right between her legs and ran his hands from her knees up to her waist, "How you doing, Lil mama?" He licked his lips before meeting Ari's gaze with his own.

Ari responded with a flirty, "I'm fine."

The stench of the Whiskey that was on his breath met her nose and immediately filled her mind with unpleasant thoughts of Lonzo. She frowned and backed away from him until her back was up against the window. "You've been drinking Whiskey."

"Yeah, you want some?" He asked.

"No, I hate the smell. It makes me sick."

He quickly dug in his pocket and pulled out a watermelon Jolly Rancher. He put it in his mouth and smiled. "My bad, Baby."

With a sly look on her face, Ari leaned back into him. This position was making her really hot and she liked it.

"Can I have a Jolly Rancher?"

He reached into his pocket, "I ain't got no mo'."

Ari pouted. He tilted his head in to kiss her and gave her the candy in his mouth. Had it not been for her playful mood, she would have thought that to be disgusting. But right now, she had no qualms.

He tugged on one of her French braids after the kiss and whispered into her ear, "I like yo' braids. You got some pretty hair."

"Thanks," she replied.

Now that she wasn't under the governance of her mother, she styled her hair in French braids all the time. It was easy to maintain. Plus, all the girls were wearing some type of braid style, even her girl Beyoncé, so she didn't feel left out.

"Won't you come back to my dorm wit' me for a lil bit?"

This was exactly what she wanted. Here she was about to use her flirtatious skills to have someone wrapped around her finger.

"Why do you want me to come back to your dorm with you?"

"Cuz it's loud in here and I wanna get to know you betta."

Ari had no intentions on going back to his dorm, but he was giving her admiration that she was desperate to receive. She decided to stall his advances until the party was over. *What did she say?* Ari thought to herself. She could have sworn she'd just heard Mischa say something about Thaddeus, but she couldn't see her through the partiers to confirm.

"What, Mischa!"

"So you gone leave wit' me or what?" The boy asked as he caressed her.

"Naw, she not," Thaddeus said.

Ari's eyes were bucked.

"Let's go, Ari."

"What are you doing here?"

"Do you want me to treat you? I will."

It didn't matter. She was already treated. The boy had no choice but to move out of the way. Thaddeus looked like he wanted to rip his head off.

He grabbed Ari's forearm yanking her off the window seals and out of the party. Ari had a mouthful to give him but she would wait until they got home. And that she did.

Fifteen minutes later they were in his condo and Ari yelled, "Why did you do that? Why did you feel you needed to come and get me? Who told you where I was?"

"I called you and you didn't answer your phone. You didn't respond to my texts either. Your last phone was out of commission. I bought you a new phone so you wouldn't have any excuses," he said sternly without matching her tone.

"Oh, so now you want to act like you care? Where's this coming from all of a sudden? You don't show me any attention! You don't care about me, you fag!"

Thaddeus snarled and ran up to Ari. He grabbed her face with one hand and pushed her so hard she flew onto the couch. The force made her dizzy. She shook her head to come to and quickly regained her composure. She was angry and ready to fight. Sure, he was about 6 feet and probably one hundred pounds heavier than she, but Ari could care less. She wanted to claw his face to bloody shreds. She rose up and he pushed her right back down, "Sit yo' immature petty a-- down!"

He knelt down in front of her and stared at her so intently that Ari's anger turned to fear.

"You won't be allowed to do what you want to do anymore. I've given you everything, and you don't appreciate it. I kept you on a loose leash for a minute to give you freedom. You don't need freedom; you need discipline."

"Women like you take nice guys like me and throw them in the sewer. You know what? I take that back. I don't think you're like them. You just don't know any better. You're still a girl. I'm going to get you right."

He stood upright and walked away. Ari set there feeling somewhat shook up. *Thaddeus doesn't seem like a woman beater, but I do deserve a good ole premeditated beatdown. What was I thinking? I can't afford to mess this up too.*

The time spent while under her mother's reign turned her into a rebellious hot head. Now, her behavior could cost her this comfy little set up. She wept and dropped her head down in shame. *This is all my fault. Where am I going to go now?* Shortly after, he came back into the living room and sat on the coffee table in front of her.

"Did I hurt you?"

She shook her head, "No". He didn't hurt her. She was just afraid he was packing her things and getting ready to kick her to the curb like Red did. Hopefully these tears, though real, would win her favor with him.

"Come here," he said.

She slowly stood up and walked towards him. He caressed her face, softly wiping away her tears.

"I'm sorry."

He stood up and kissed her lips. "Stop crying."

She kissed him back and allowed him to lead her into the bedroom. Ari's heart beat rapidly. She'd been complaining about his unwillingness to touch her and now she was as terrified as a virgin.

He took off her shirt, unzipped her jeans and pulled them down. He fully undressed himself. His sculpted body was marked with tattoos, and the sight of it sprinkled her insides with waves of arousal. He pressed against her as they fell onto the bed.

Ari's breathing was jagged. She held her eyes closed. No longer did she feel so sure of herself once he pulled off her panties and put his whole mouth on her dandelion.

She'd never felt this kind of sensation before and it was driving her crazy. She tried to scoot away from him but he firmly gripped her hips and held her still. She let out a wail when his tongue invaded her walls until he felt she was ready to accept his manliness.

That night Thaddeus ravaged her little body and showed her honeycomb no mercy. She lay in bed motionless underneath the covers with her back towards him. He grabbed all of her braids and gently pulled her head back,

"You still think I'm a fag now?"

QUEEN ARI
"Hmph…what a beautiful surprise."

"Get up Ari and make breakfast."

Thaddeus pulled back the blinds causing the sun to shine right through the window like a flashlight onto Ari's face. She yawned and stretched underneath the covers.

"What did you say?" She managed to ask through a second yawn.

"I said get up and make breakfast."

Ari sat up in bed and rubbed sleep out of her eyes. She watched Thaddeus, who was fully dressed, walk out of the bedroom. *He usually cooks us breakfast though. Why do I have to do that now?* She thought back to what Mischa told her yesterday about how a man changes once he has sex with a woman. *Is that it? Is he really changing or is this my punishment for last night?*

She got out of bed and put on some loungewear and house shoes, before strolling into the kitchen. Thaddeus had left for his morning jog. On the island were bags of groceries. He must have gone to the store while she was being a sleeping beauty. Needless to say, she was in no mood to be Susie homemaker and even if she was, she couldn't even boil water.

She reached into the bags and pulled out all the food he'd bought: bacon, eggs, margarine, orange juice, and pancake mix. She picked up the box of pancake mix first and looked on the back of the box for the instructions.

Pour a cup or two into a mixing boil. Mix with water or milk.
Stir until mix is no longer lumpy. Add more water or milk for
thinner pancakes. Is he serious?

She smacked her lips and sighed.

About forty-five minutes later, Thaddeus returned
wiping sweat off of his face with a towel and came into the
kitchen to find Ari cleaning up her mess. The only thing
she managed to cook right was the bacon. Thaddeus
looked over at the stove and then at the empty table.

"So what happened?"

"I couldn't flip the pancakes over and they kept sticking.
And I couldn't crack the eggs right. The shells kept falling
in the skillet! Why couldn't you cook breakfast like you
usually do? You know I don't know how to cook," Ari said,
throwing the oven mitten on the counter. She was beyond
frustrated.

Thaddeus stared at her with an absent expression for a
minute and then started laughing.

"You better learn how to if you want to stay in my
house."

He brushed past her and picked up the box of pancake
mix before shaking the container, "Did you really screw up
a half box of pancake mix?"

Ari was about to plead her case but he stopped her
before she could open her mouth, "Get out my kitchen."

***

"Ari, if you don't come out of that bathroom, I'm going to lock you in it and leave you here," Thaddeus yelled from the living room.

"Ok, I'm coming! My hair isn't acting right. It's ugly."

"Just put it in a ponytail."

She was not about to slap a ponytail on her head for her pre-birthday celebration, but her frizzy hair was definitely battling her patience. Thaddeus tried to convince her to get a relaxer but she refused. She was scared it would eat her hair up like it did to all the girls she knew in high school. One minute they had hair like Rapunzel and the next their hair was like Kunta Kente from Roots. The thought made her crack up and shake her head. Her amusement was cut short when the rat-tail comb got stuck in her hair. She sat on the tub and let out a scream.

Thaddeus rushed into the bathroom, "What's wrong with you?'

"My stupid hair!"

"Are you going to cancel this dinner then?"

Cancelling dinner would have been something he wanted. Despite his protest, Ari really wanted to go to the Cheesecake Factory because she'd never been. She also invited Mischa and Prentice to join. Thaddeus, however, was not a fan of double dating. Maybe it had to do with his age.

"So what are you going to do then? You're going to sit there and be a brat? I really don't have the patience for your antics, Ari," Thaddeus said before leaving the bathroom.

He'd been fussing at her all day today, about everything. He made her clean up the entire condo and had something to say about each thing she did, including laundry. She felt like Cinderella. If only she hadn't made him so mad the day before, her life would still be kosher and simple.

After kung fu gripping the rat-tail comb from her massive mane, Ari reluctantly styled her hair into a high bun. She had to do something before Thaddeus canceled their plans.

***

"So are they still coming?" Thaddeus impatiently asked Ari.

Mischa and Prentice had yet to arrive to the Cheesecake Factory, and they were now over thirty minutes late. Ari didn't want to order anything before they came, which only irritated Thaddeus.

"Mischa's not answering her phone, Thaddeus. Let's wait just a few more minutes," she told him.

"No," he said.

"What?"

"I said, no. I'm paying for this, so I'm ordering. What do you want?"

"I'm going to wait."

"Pick up the menu and figure out what you want. We are not waiting on them. If you wait you will have to pay for your own meal!"

Ari frowned. He was being a jerk. "That's fine; I can pay for my meal."

Thaddeus gave her an evil glare and got up from the table.

"Where are you going?"

He said nothing as he walked away. After a few minutes, Ari inhaled deeply before taking her phone out of her clutch to call him.

"Where are you going, Thaddeus?"

"Home, Ari. You can pay for your meal, right? You can also pay for a cab home. I hope they don't show. Then, you'll be eating dinner alone, which is exactly what you deserve. And you better be home by 10 o'clock or I'm putting the burglar alarm on."

He hung up before she could respond. It was now close to 8 p.m. *Excuse me? What does he mean 10 o'clock? This must be his slick way of giving me a curfew and trying to tighten his so-called leash? Wow! He has some nerve!*

She was not feeling that for one second. *Who does he think he is? I'm about to be nineteen years old in less than two days!* But where on Earth would she go if she broke curfew?

"Hey, Ari."

A text popped up on her phone.

Confused, Ari responded to the message, "Hey. Who is this?"

"Guess."

"Ummm, yeah I give up. Lol"

"It's Evey."

Ari's heartbeat thumped uncontrollably. Suddenly, all of the memories of her early teenage years flooded into her mind. The last time she spoke to Evey was via their usual email exchange a few weeks ago. She was excited to share that she finally had a cell phone and gave Evey her new number. But Evey never used it. She figured they'd just grown apart.

She responded, "Evey! How are you? I really miss you, Sister!"

"Hey, I'm sorry but Prentice is under the weather. We won't be making it to dinner. Forgive us! Love you, honey bunches!" Mischa's text unexpectedly interrupted her conversation with Evey. By now, Mischa was infamous for pulling no-shows, so Ari wasn't at all that surprised. She didn't even respond to her. Luckily, Evey deterred her from a potential tantrum.

"I miss you too Girlie. I just moved back to Chicago. By the way, Happy Birthday, Babes! I want to see you soon!"

"Seriously? You're actually here? Where are you now?"

"I'm staying downtown for a little while."

"I'm downtown! What's your address?"

Evey gave Ari her address, and Ari was at her front door within a half hour. Evey still had the same peachy skin and gorgeous smile; she had not changed a bit. She was wearing her hair in long box braids. The two girls embraced and cried as soon as Evey opened the door. They both laughed momentarily because the reunion reminded them of the scene in Color Purple when Nettie came back from Africa to see Celie.

"So, what's been going on with you, Evey? How's your mom?"

"She's doing really well. She's finally married and truly happy."

"Aw, that's great! I'm really glad to hear that. Especially after…."

Ari's voice trailed off and her mind was bombarded with images of Estavian. She thought about the way her heart broke that day, and how devastated Evey and her Mom had been. These images were gracefully pushed aside by Evey's gentle call:

"Ari…are you okay?"

"Yeah, I'm fine. Anyway, what made you come back to Chicago? Are you going to go to school up here?"

"I wanted to come back home. I really missed Chicago and I missed my best friend. I guess since I finally healed from the past, I'm able to move forward with my life. And yeah, I'm going to finish at Columbia with you."

Before a cloud of grief could sweep over her again, the news of Evey attending Columbia gave her a boost of joy. Her best friend was officially back to stay. Even though she really didn't feel like she had any good news to share with Evey, she participated in the catch up and reminisced right along with her. She made sure she told Evey about her current dealings with an older man, whom she was now living with, and about the curfew that was enacted tonight.

"Oh wow, he's tripping. Well I don't mind you staying over here. In fact, I'd rather you did. It'll be like the old days when you used to come over to our house to get away from home for a while. So you know what that means? Sleepover!"

Ari giggled and smiled at her friend. Evey was always so jovial and lighthearted, even in the most difficult situations. She seemed free of all her past hurts. Ari looked at her best friend admiringly and thought, *I wish I could be healed too, Evey. I just don't know where or how to begin.* If she would be honest with herself, she'd been running from her pain like it was a contagious virus. It's funny how a lot of things changed, while so many others stayed the same. That fragile, insecure, younger teenager had emerged from the murky depths of her soul on the eve of her 19h birthday. How ironic for this ghost of a bruised past to arrive when it wasn't even invited.

"Hmph…what a beautiful surprise," whispered Ari.

125

QUEEN ARI
"… like thorns ripping through her flesh."

December

It was a week before Christmas and it'd barely snowed at all. School was out for winter break, and almost everyone Ari was well acquainted with was going back home. Mischa dropped out of college shortly after Prentice left to go to the Police Academy. Ari didn't agree with her decision and the two of them got into a heated argument about it. Ari had to accept the fact that Mischa was her own person and was responsible for her own actions and decisions. It was hard to do because she knew her friend was making a huge mistake, but she didn't want to jeopardize their friendship by pushing the issue.

Evey continued to study at Columbia. She also decided to stay in Chicago instead of going back to Atlanta for the holidays. Ari's situation was a little more complicated. Thaddeus had talked her out of living in the dorms so she could stay with him fulltime. Now, Ari wished she hadn't made that choice because he was no longer the man she once knew. He demanded she cook for him, clean the house, and arrive home by her new curfew time of 9p.m. Thaddeus had become manipulative, controlling, and sexually aggressive. He wanted her when and how he wanted. And if she denied him, he would threaten to kick her out.

By November, she barely saw him during the week because his shift had changed at the nuclear power plant he worked for outside of Chicago so he required a lot of her attention on the weekends.

If she wanted to hang out with Evey and Mischa, he would take all of her shoes and lock them in his trunk. He even threw her phone in the toilet and refused to pay for a replacement. His behavior forced her to start saving all of her money from her job at Starbucks. The plan was to move out and possibly stay with Evey until she was able to afford her own place. Ari decided that she was to never depend on a man for anything again. A month later, her situation had only worsened. It was getting old and slowly unscrewing her mental stability.

"So Mischa, what time is your flight?" Evey asked.

"7:30 in the morning."

"Ok. You should just go get your luggage and stay the night here so we can drop you off at the airport," Evey told her.

Ari was glad that Evey and Mischa hit it off. They were her family since she didn't really have or know of anybody in her bloodline except for her demented mother. For Ari, this time of the year was always the hardest for two reasons: it always resurfaced the pain from the death of her first love and her estrangement from her mother made her feel unwanted. She found herself eating takeout every holiday and crying herself to sleep. She hoped that this Christmas would be different because Evey was here now. Evey had a huge family and was planning on visiting almost of all of them since she was in Chicago to stay. Ari was in no mood for takeout this year; she wanted some real food for a change. Most of all, she wanted to be around some loving people.

"I'm mad neither one of y'all noticed anything different about me,' Mischa said.

"What happened?" Ari asked.

"Yeah what did we miss, girl?" Evey asked.

Mischa held up her left hand and showed off a sparkly engagement ring.

"Oh my God! Mischa you're getting married!" Ari exclaimed, clearly surprised.

"I am! Prentice proposed to me at David Buster's last night," Mischa beamed.

"Awww, congratulations Honey," Evey cheered.

The three girls gushed over Mischa's ring and talked about wedding gowns and how different her life would be after becoming a wife. Ari applauded every woman who became a wife. She vowed to never get married because her life just seemed too jacked up to share it with someone else. But she was really happy for Mischa.

Mischa left a little while later and told them she'd be back with her luggage. Ari and Evey decided to go Christmas shopping at Marshall Fields. They laughed a lot, tried on tons of clothes, made fun of a host of people, and simply enjoyed each other's company. On their way back to Evey's place, Ari broke down. Snapshots of where she came from, where she was right now, and where she could be attacked her mind like thorns ripping through her flesh. She didn't like her life; she was miserable inside. Happiness was temporary. Joy was an enigma.

"I see you're finally ready to talk about it. I'm listening," said Evey as she wrapped her arm around her friend's shoulder. "

"You knew?" Asked Ari, in between sobs.

"Of course I did. I wouldn't be your best friend if I didn't. Now, tell me what's really going on here," Evey replied, giving Ari's shoulder a reassuring squeeze.

"I'm not happy, Evey. I try to be happy but it just seems so unnatural. I want to be free like you are. I feel like I'm missing something, and it's been gone for a very long time. Life just doesn't seem like it's worth living. Nothing has ever worked in my favor. I've always gotten leftovers. Always."

"No don't say that, Ari. You may not have been dealt with what appears to be a fair hand but you've been dealt one nonetheless. It's up to you to play your cards right. And if you don't like them, you can get new ones. Who said you had to keep playing with them?"

Oh, Evey. That is so much easier said than done, thought Ari. *How do you get new cards after being dealt crappy ones and feeling like you've been forced to play them forever? Who was the ultimate cardholder?*

"Ari, you should come to church with me on Sunday. It's my auntie's church and we would love to have you. You need to be introduced to God. I know you know of him, but you need to get to know him for yourself. God is the only reason that I've been able to cope with life's ups and downs. You know I haven't always been dealt a fair hand either, but he taught me how to play my cards the best way that I can."

Did she say church? I'll pass. Ari inhaled and exhaled slowly before wiping her face. The thought of church was beyond unappealing. Her mother always told her that Christianity was a white man's religion. She said that's why all the paintings of Jesus were of a white man and told Ari that no other race had a right to worship Him. If Ari could recall, however, her mother was a faithful churchgoer when Ari was around five probably at the time her dad disappeared.

She remembered her mother in the living room balling, "Them church people burned me. They burned me." She always thought her mother meant that she was literally burned with fire. That thought alone made her turn down Evey's offer.

A few hours had passed. Thaddeus was blowing her phone up. It was Friday, so he expected her to be home in another hour to either A. Cook him dinner, B. Have sex with him, Or C. all of the above. She could care less if he threatened to kick her out. She had a way of escape now. Mischa was the person she was waiting to hear from anyway. She should have been back to Evey's place by now.

"You should call Mischa, Ari and see where she is," Evey said yawning.

It was almost 9 o'clock. Ari was sleepy too. They'd been up since the wee hours of the morning. She called and heard someone pick up but she didn't hear anything besides muffled moans.

"Mischa?"

Moans.

"Mischa, are you ok? What's the matter?"

Click.

Ari frowned and called her back but it went straight to voicemail. She looked at Evey, who had an alarmed look on her face.

"What did she say?"

"Nothing, really. I just heard moans."

"Moans? Did she sound hurt?"

"Maybe she and Prentice were "congregating" and I just so happened to call in on the action," Ari said as they burst into a fit of laughter.

"Alright girl, I'm going to go. I guess Prentice will be taking her to the airport then."

"Ok, Babes. Call me when you get home. Love you."

Ari and Evey hugged before parting ways. Ari flagged a cab and rode back to the condo. To her surprise, the burglar alarm didn't go off when she opened the door. Thaddeus hadn't set it apparently.

Thank God.

It was a quarter to ten, way past her 9 o'clock curfew. If he asked why she was late, she would lie and say that she hadn't gotten used to the curfew change. She kicked off her shoes at the door and sat her purse in the closet. The house was dark. Thaddeus must have decided to go out or something. She was relieved. She didn't feel like being bothered with his shenanigans or tirades tonight.

"So you still think you can do what the hell you want to do huh?"

His deep voice piercing through the darkness scared her out of her skin. She gasped.

"Thaddeus? What are you doing sitting without any lights on?"

"Answer my question, Ari."

"I for---"

"You didn't forget! Don't lie to me dammit! You think I'm joking with you. I called you a million times today. Where were you?"

He didn't give her a chance to respond. He took a fist full of her hair and slung her into the bedroom.

"When I call, you answer! When I text, you respond! When I say something, you listen! You little hardheaded skank!"

131

Ari was scrambling across the bed to get away from him but he grabbed her leg. This entire interaction reminded her so much of the two occasions Lonzo tried to rape her. Her entire body trembled with terror. Thaddeus literally ripped her jeans off and forced her into bed straddling her.

"No please Thaddeus! Please! You don't have to take it! I'll give it you! I'll give it to you! Please don't hurt me!"

"You don't tell me what to do! You hear me?" Thaddeus lifted up his hand and smacked her face. It stunned her more than it hurt. This was the first time he ever actually hit her and she wasn't sure how to respond.

"You're spoiled. You don't listen. You run over me. I'm going to show you that you can't run over me. I'm in control of you."

She could feel warm fluid oozing out of her nose; it was more than likely blood. Sadly, her nose was used to this abuse. It had been awhile though. Thaddeus was too strong for her to fight him so she just gave up.

He snatched her shirt over her head and turned her over on her stomach. She begin to squirm. He wrapped his entire forearm around her neck, placing her into a chokehold. Ari cried as the blood from her nose seeped into her mouth. She was struggling to breathe. He invaded her woman cave with full force and raped her from behind while she gasped for air. The pain of his forceful entry was excruciating. Ari tried to fight again, but it only made Thaddeus tighten his hold on her neck like a boa constrictor.

"You better take this like the woman you think you are."

Ari wailed in pain softly as she was being violated. Then she blacked out.

PART 2

QUEEN ARI
"It was as if her mind was going through a purge…"

March 2010

"The first time I contemplated suicide was when I was 10 years old. My mother had just beaten me black and blue and for some reason I thought I could wash the bruises away by taking a bath. So, I ran some bath water and tried to scrub away the evidence of her hatred for me. But it didn't work. The thought of death seemed so euphoric that I deemed death my Prince Charming. I slowly allowed my body to slide down into the water until I was completely submerged.

I was only under for a few moments before my mother burst into the bathroom with a lit cigarette in her mouth and sat down on the toilet to pee. She spoke very calmly, as if she knew exactly what I was I trying to do. She said, "You know people who kill themselves go straight to hell, right?" And just like that, she wiped herself, flushed the toilet, and left out."

Ari couldn't believe she was spilling her guts to a complete stranger. She'd managed to tell this person everything, including the story about her being raped by a past lover but for some reason her thoughts suddenly drifted back to when she was a little girl. It was as if her mind was going through a purge and ridding itself of everything toxic.

To all who knew her, Ari's life seemed to be perfect. She graduated from Columbia University Summa Cum Laude with a Bachelor's in Business and Art. She'd received national recognition for her paintings before and after obtaining her degree. She even snagged numerous grants that afforded her the ability to purchase property in Bronzeville, where her art studio and gallery now stood. God was finally welcomed into her life, and she became an active member of the church that her best friend Evey attended. To everyone else, she was twenty-three years old with nothing but an abundant life ahead of her.

Yet even still, she secretly suffered from long bouts of depression. Night terrors tormented her. Insomnia prevented her sleep. How could it be that God delivered her out of the hell she'd lived in but seemed to overlook the hell that was inside of her? After talking to her pastor about how she was feeling, he suggested she seek professional counseling. Evey's mother referred her to Dr. Isaiah Sinclair, a reputable Christian psychologist in Atlanta. Because she'd never been to Atlanta, she decided to make the trip and give Dr. Sinclair a try.

Ari hated revisiting the pain from her past, but she knew it was necessary. Resting on a comfortable chaise lounge with her eyes closed, Ari finally exhaled a sigh of relief. She'd gotten past the hardest parts of her life in a little over an hour.

"You say that was the first time you thought about suicide, Ari. So there have been other times then?"

"Yeah. The thoughts always come when I feel like I'm losing control. I know I shouldn't think about that. Especially since I believe in God, but I do. Those words my mother spoke about suicide all those years ago always haunt me.

You know, about going to hell if you commit suicide? I thought about something though, how does anybody know you go to hell? Who actually killed themselves and came back to tell about it? I mean, I've never seen it say that in the Bible. Who knows what really happens to you? It really doesn't matter to me one way or the other. I just don't understand, why? Why do I feel like this?"

"Ari, you're going to have to understand that these thoughts of death are generic thoughts that have been sold to you by the devil. Your past has opened up small slots for the devil to advertise these disgusting thoughts to your mind, and they've been appealing because you haven't taken the time to truly deal with your pain. But they're not really how you feel. The enemy wants you to believe that suicide is the only way out because he knows your past is your weakness. He can't attack or tempt you in any other way because you're secure in those areas. He's only going to invade those places where you're most vulnerable. These places, as we now know, are rooted in your past."

Ari sat straight up and looked Dr. Sinclair directly in his face. He looked back at her, as he adjusted his glasses. His young face was serious but friendly. She wanted to rebuke his last statement but knew that he spoke the truth. God must have needed a voice to get to her today because he definitely used Dr. Sinclair.

"So, what happens now? I just don't know what to do. I feel hopeless and helpless Dr. Sinclair. How do I get rid of these thoughts?"

Dr. Sinclair gave her a broad bright expression, as if he were waiting on her to ask.

"Ari, you're going to have to reconcile with your past. My father- in- law said it this way, you can't get passed your past until you get over your past."

"Whatever you don't confront, you can't get over."

Ari turned up her lips in confusion. She'd never heard of such a thing.

"What does that mean exactly?"

"You have to look at your past directly in its face and forgive it for all that it has done to you. This means you're going to have to forgive your mother. You're going to have to forgive your father. You're going to have to forgive Red and Thaddeus. You're even going to have to forgive the person who killed your first love. All the actors of your past must be forgiven. That includes you, Ari," he paused and looked at her for emphasis before speaking again.

"This will inevitably start a domino effect in your psyche. You take down all the giants in your head, one smooth stone and slingshot at a time. Cast down all those ungodly imaginations wreaking havoc in your mind, and you will finally receive the freedom that you so deserve. Does that make any sense?"

Ari bit her bottom lip as she took it all in. After a moment, she answered, "Yeah, it actually does," she said before a frown spread across her face. "Wait, so does that mean I have to find these people?"

"I don't recommend that you find Red and Thaddeus because it's not necessary, but I do believe that you should reconnect with your mother and father. It will make moving forward a little easier for you. You can do it, Ari. I have faith in you. You've come entirely too far to let this stop you."

She was glad he had faith in her because she surely didn't have faith in herself. She sat there for a minute and looked out the window. *Is this really happening? I haven't seen my mother in years. What am I going to say after all this time?*

The task ahead of her was daunting but for some reason she felt a sense of reassurance and relief. *What are you thinking, Ari? Remember Philippians 4:13; you got this!* Life suddenly seemed trouble free for a minute. She had finally been given the green light she needed to release the burden of her past. She was enlightened and relieved.

"You have a little more time on the clock, Ari. Did you want to go back to the incident involving your sexual assault?"

"Uh, no. We can talk about it tomorrow," Ari replied. She needed some alone time to register all that she'd released this afternoon and all that she'd received from Dr. Sinclair.

"Ok that sounds good. Well, Ari I'm glad you came. It was a bit surprising to learn that you passed up so many therapists in Chicago though," he said.

"I know right. But hey, when God gives you specific instructions, you have to abide by them. Plus my best friend Evey, had so many good things to say about you."

"Great! Let's pray before you leave," Dr. Sinclair said before coming from around his desk.

He grabbed her hands and held them tightly. They bowed their heads and he prayed, "Heavenly Father, we just thank you for your grace and for your mercy. We also thank you for deliverance, Father God. We thank you for making known to us the pathway of life. We thank you for being a present help in the time of trouble.

God, I ask that you take care of your daughter, Ari. Cover her mind and fill it with pure thoughts. Help her to think on things above and not below. Touch her heart as well, Father. Create in her a clean heart and renew in her a right spirit. Give her all the tools she needs for reconciliation and ready her spirit to forgive. For you said, in your word, that you can't forgive us if we can't forgive our fellow man. Let this be the key that unlocks the door of her peace, happiness, and that more abundantly. Lastly, I pray that you give her even more strength and courage to come back here to see me tomorrow. In Jesus' name we do pray, amen."

"Amen."

"So, same time tomorrow right?"

"Yes. Thank you so much. I really appreciated this session."

"You're welcome. I believe you're on the right track."

Shortly after saying goodbye to Dr. Sinclair, Ari drove her rental car back to her hotel in downtown Atlanta. Once inside her room, she ordered a chicken Caesar salad through room service.

She took a seat on the rose colored divan by the window of her hotel room to reflect. Weights slid off her shoulders as she replayed the much needed and long overdue therapy session.

Even though she was an active member in her church, she admitted that she prayed sparingly, so she took this time to get on her knees to pray.

"God, you brought me here so that I could release myself from the hurt and pain of my past. Now you want me to turn around and confront it. I don't even know how to do that, but I'm going to try.

You want me to find my mother and my father? Show me where to look and I will go. I need your help God. I can't do this in my own my strength. Please help me. In Jesus' name. Amen."

Ari got up from her knees and pulled the Bible out of the nightstand near the side of the bed. One of the pages was folded in half and verse Isaiah 61:1 was partially circled with a highlighter. She read the verse,

"To appoint them that mourn in Zion, to give them a crown of beauty for ashes, the oil of joy for mourning, the garment of praise for the spirit of heaviness; that they might be called trees of righteousness, the planting of the Lord, that he might be glorified."

Shortly after her meal arrived, she ate and imagined herself digesting the scripture she'd read.

QUEEN ARI
"This was the ungodly hour ..."

"Hi, how are you?"

"Hi. I'm, I'm fine. How are you?'

"I'm great. My name is Carter. What's your name?"

Ari stood in the middle of a produce store staring at a man who literally had the power to turn her into a pull of mushy goo. His skin was like new tar and his eyes that were shaded by his baseball cap were jovial. He arrested all of her good senses with his introduction. His tall stature made him look down at her.

"My name's Ari," she finally responded.

He took her hand firmly and shook it. His gaze was mesmerizing.

"So, I didn't mean to bother you, but I saw you when you walked into the store. I was already in line though. I paid for my groceries and came back to look for you. I think I went down almost every aisle until I found you here," he stated.

"Aw, is that right?" Ari blushed. She was flattered.

"I want to get to know you. You want to hang out with me sometime?" Carter asked.

Ari pursed her lips. She hesitated momentarily. She hadn't been out with a guy in some time. All kinds of nerves tackled her. She quickly relaxed her reservations and exchanged numbers with him.

Ari found herself being pulled into a very tumultuous six-month love affair with Carter after this innocent exchange. She discovered in the third month of their rendezvous, that he'd been married for two years and had a baby on the way.

No matter how many times his wife would call her and threaten to rip her bottom from her torso, she still somehow believed that he would eventually leave this woman, for her. She ran away with the thoughts that this man would marry her. She often daydreamed about having children with him, copying and pasting his and her features to breathe life into her imaginary offspring. She went as far as creating names for them and entertained the reveries of Carter being a perfect dad to them and a loving husband to her.

This dream was shattered the day after she and Carter got into one of many confrontations. She gave him an ultimatum and told him they could no longer be together if he didn't make a decision to leave his wife. To prove his undying love for Ari, he called his wife right in front of her and told his wife he wanted a divorce. Ari was shocked but happy at the same time. Yet the next day, while on her way to a meeting downtown she saw he and his wife walking hand in hand towards Millennium Park. She felt heartbroken and betrayed. He'd lied to her, yet again.

Buzz Buzz

Ari's phone vibrated on the nightstand next to her interrupting her mental backtracking as she lay awake. She reached for her phone and looked to see she'd received a text message. The time was 3:46 a.m.

"I'm on my way."

It was Carter.

It had been close to two months since she'd seen him.

She was determined to leave him alone for good. But a moment of weakness prior to boarding her flight here to Atlanta caused her to reach out to him. She wasn't expecting him to follow her here though. Now she lay in bed in this hotel room full of regret. She wished she hadn't accepted his invitation to come see her.

She jumped out of bed and ran into the bathroom to disrobe. She pulled her hair up into a bun and stepped into the shower. After bathing, she dried herself and lathered her body in her lavender Oil of Olay lotion. Not too long after drying her face, she heard a knock at the door. Her heart thumped violently. If she was full of shame and anxiety prior to him knocking, her arousal choked it all before she made it to the door to open it.

There he was, an ornament of the devil covered in dark chocolate with a smile laced with deception. She let him in and he wasted no time as he pulled the towel off of her. He grabbed her hair with his left hand and pulled her head back. He began to kiss and bite her neck and it was as if her body was engulfed in flames. He then pulled her into him and allowed her to pull his shirt up to his muscular shoulders and over his head. She then unbuckled his pants and helped him take them off.

Once he was completely naked, he picked her up and wrapped her legs around him to walk to the bed. This was the ungodly hour she'd convinced herself she would never partake in again. Yet she'd given in to temptation because she wanted love, even if it was on discount.

***

"Wake up! Wake up! What's wrong with you!"
Ari looked up to see her mother rushing out her room.

"Momma wait! Wait! where are you going? Don't leave yet! I need to talk to you! Don't leave," Ari screamed.

She jumped up from her resting place in the bed. She'd been dreaming. If she could admit she hadn't dreamed of anything for quite some time. She was somewhat glad about it too. Those dreams did nothing but annoy her at most. Seeing her mother in her dream irritated her all the more. Carter woke up and turned over to face her.

"You had a nightmare or something?"

Ari smirked. She got up out of the bed and drew the shades allowing the sun to invade the dark room where illegal passions parlayed the night before. Ari put on her black baby-doll gown and long mesh robe. She stood looking out at the beautiful setting and wondered how her life still seemed like a ball of ugly mess.

"What's the matter baby? Why don't you come back over here with me? Maybe we can go for round two," Carter solicited.

Ari felt a sickness similar to those few times she suffered from a hangover during her time in college. She unlocked the door to the balcony and stepped outside. The breeze was soothing to her skin.

Today was April 1st. *The day of fools, how ironic.* She exhaled, and wondered how did sin smell to God. How did sin smell on someone he'd pulled out of all kinds of gruesome situations? How did sin smell on someone who he'd heard time and time again worship him in his house? She held her head down and let her tears fall.

"I'm sorry God. I really am. I don't want to live like this."

Carter came behind her and massaged her shoulders. He seductively kissed her neck. He'd memorized the places on her body that disarmed her. This time though, Ari decided not to accept his advances. She took his hands off her shoulders and turned to face him.

"Go home, to your wife Carter. I don't want to see you anymore," she spoke with a calm sincerity.

"What?"

"I'm about to get in the shower. When I get out I don't want to see you here," she told him.

She brushed passed him and walked into the room to go to the bathroom. She closed the bathroom door, locked it, and sat on the sink. Shortly after, Carter jiggled the doorknob of the bathroom door.

"Ari, so that's how you feel? I flew all the way out here for you and you gone treat me like this?"

Ari wanted to respond to him but she didn't. *You're not worth it.* He was a dog and she willingly became his bag of Kibbles and Bits. The path with him was leading her to a place she knew all to well: hell! She let her fingers gallop on the counter while she waited for Carter to leave. *Oh my God, he's taking his jolly ole time!* Ari's bottom went numb. She assumed he was probably hoping she would come out. The door finally slammed hard enough to give her the assurance that he'd departed.

***

"Good afternoon, Ari."

"Good afternoon, Dr. Sinclair."

This was day two of her therapy session with him. Ari didn't know what to expect.

Yesterday did not really go as planned for her. Overtime, she'd become a hoarder of her traumatic experiences, so much so she'd compartmentalized what she would share and what she wouldn't share with Dr. Sinclair. But he had a way with counseling her that literally forced her to let go of all her inhibitions. Her heart and mind betrayed her and willingly gave this man all the keys to the hidden vaults within her. Today, she was pretty much prepared to be caught off guard, again.

"How are you feeling," Dr. Sinclair asked.

Ari exhaled, "I'm nervous."

"You shouldn't be nervous. I know this may be hard for you, Ari. But I want you to know that everything you share with me, will stay here. You're safe. You can let your guards down. You don't have to be in control," Dr. Sinclair told her.

His voice was paternal. She closed her eyes and breathed in and out. She hadn't even said but a few words and he was working his medicine.

"Ari sit back and lay down. You can even take your shoes off if you want to. Get comfortable. You don't have to know what's going to happen next. Take a sip of uncertainty. If you knew everything, you wouldn't need God. I want you to whisper this, I need you God."

"I need you God. I need you God. I need you God," she complied with his polite directives.

The room was quiet for a moment until some soft worship music began to play. She had never really heard this kind of music before. She was used to the upbeat gospel songs and old hymns. This was different. It felt like washing your face with cool water on a humid day.

"Now Ari, we're going to go back to the night you were first sexually assaulted by Thaddeus. What emotion did you feel most?"

Balls of tears bum rushed her eyes.

"I felt scared."

"What or who came to your mind?"

She hesitated for a moment and exhaled once more before telling him, "My daddy."

"Why?"

"Because...I don't know."

"Of course you know Ari. All of the things and people that could have come to mind, while this man overpowered you and took something of you without permission, yet your father is the person you thought of, why?"

"He was never there when I needed him. When I needed him to save me. When I needed him to protect me. I wish he were there. I just wish..."

Ari wailed and curled up on the plush sofa. Her back faced Dr. Sinclair.

"Go ahead and let it all out. This pain is like a stuffed animal that you've been holding on to for too long. It's old and raggedy. It's not serving any purpose. Just imagine, God standing before you with a brand new stuffed toy waiting for you to exchange it with what you have. Give it to him Ari. Tell me, how did this affect your relationship with men after your rape?"

She sniffed and returned back to her original position on her back. Hard breaths pushed from her lungs like an exhaust pipe on a car.

As she pondered about his last question, Dr. Sinclair turned off the worship music and got up from his seat. He walked to a Keurig machine sitting on a table on the opposite side of his office and made her some tea. He walked over to her and handed her the dark blue teacup. She sat up and blew a few times over the hot liquid and he went back to his seat.

The first sip of the tea was delightful. The flavor excited her palate. "What kind of tea is this?" She asked.

"It's peach tea by Bigelow. It's my favorite. My fiancée actually makes it for me from time to time with real peaches. Hers tastes better. But you know, I don't have that kind of time to peel peaches and make tea," he laughed at himself.

Ari joined his amusement. The lighthearted moment felt good.

"I take it that's your fiancée on that picture?"

"Yes. Yes that's my lovely fiancée Naomi. She's a treasure in my life."

Ari stared at Dr. Sinclair. He seemed to escape momentarily somewhere probably where his fiancée was. An affable expression rested on his slim face. She marveled him as his Versace eyeglasses showcased his dancing eyes. *He's in love with his fiancée.* Then, a woebegone garland sat on the door of Ari's heart.

"I don't think I'm lovable, Dr. Sinclair."

Dr. Sinclair responded to her statement by snapping out of his own commercial break.

"Why do you believe this about yourself Ari?"

"I'm so damaged. What man in his right mind would love someone like me?"

"Is this how you enter into relationships with men?"

"Yeah. I think so. It's like, I hide my vulnerabilities and I kind of sabotage my relationships by just having sex with them. Sometimes I don't even want to have sex, I just do it as a way to have someone to lay next to me without fully revealing all of myself. It's my way of controlling the situation. I want to be loved but on my terms. I guess I just figured if they knew all of me and saw all of me they wouldn't want to love me so I just settle for superficial love."

"What's the longest relationship you've been in with a man?"

"My first love, the one who was killed. It was about a year. All the others I never recorded the time. They never made it a year, I know for sure. I usually ended it before it could get that far."

"Ari, I need you to understand something. As long as you live in fear of being seen for who you really are, you will never experience true love. John 3:16, I'm sure you're familiar with, says that, "For God so loved the world that he gave his only begotten son so that whoever would believe in him should have everlasting life." That everlasting life, is filled with joy, peace, happiness, and true agape love. God doesn't want you to hide behind all that pain and heartache. If so the gift of his son Jesus dying on the cross for you would have been done in vain. You deserve love and not bootlegged love or love orchestrated by your own standards. Ari you need to allow yourself first to experience God's unconditional love."

Ari chewed on that revelation about experiencing everlasting life. It was much different from what she was used to. She'd always thought it meant to live forever which never made sense to her.

Dr. Sinclair's explanation however, sparked a paradigm shift. She looked back at the picture of Dr. Sinclair and his fiancée. His fiancée was so beautiful. She had a perfect smile and magnetic eyes. She looked like she had not a care in the world. No baggage or drama. She looked free.

"You want freedom. Freedom is what you will also find in God's love."

"How did you do that? How did you know that's what I was thinking?" She asked completely bewildered.

"I saw it in your face, Ari. Your aches and pains enslave you. You don't think you deserve to be loved by man because you don't even believe you are a suitable candidate to be loved by God. That's your issue. You think because of all the things that has happened to you from childhood to recent is indicative of what God has to offer you. God was in the midst keeping you while you suffered but none of these things were his portion for you. And that's what I meant earlier when I spoke of the stuffed animal you have as oppose to what he has. He's been waiting on you to acknowledge that you can have more than what you've ever received. But he's not going to force you to take it. You have to want it."

"But Dr. Sinclair, I didn't even know he had anything for me. How was I supposed to know?" Ari was frustrated. But then she was reminded of the time she had some artifacts delivered to her art gallery that came all the way from Nairobi, Africa.

She'd missed its drop off and for some reason she never received the notification from the currier that the package had come. So almost two weeks had passed and an art curator in Nairobi emailed her and asked if she'd received the gift he sent to her.

Confused, she let him know she hadn't gotten anything. To her surprise, after researching and investigating, she'd missed every attempt made by the currier to sign for the gift, so it was in transit back to Africa.

"God tried to reach out to me a few time to let me know didn't he?"

"Yep. You got it."

"He always does. Even though he's not going to force his love on you, he drops hints to let you know his love is available for full enjoyment. But we're often distracted with life and our own tastes and desires. Sometimes the various things we involve ourselves in whether it's work, project deadlines, future goals, relationships, don't matter they can sometimes keep us from catching those hints. The hints usually come right after some kind of an upset, a failure, or a breakup. That's when God comes in with a reminder that he has something better, something that's been on reserve for you since you were in your mother's womb. Isn't that amazing?"

"It really is Dr. Sinclair. Wow!"

Ari sat in awe. Another layer of shackles were falling off of her.

"Ari I want you to continue to reflect on this new revelation about God's love and your unrestricted access to it. Now, tomorrow for your final session I want you to go back to your hotel room and write a letter to your mother and your father separately. We're going to talk about forgiveness and how to move forward. Ok?"

Ari felt a little tense about that idea but she would complete her homework assignment nonetheless.

QUEEN ARI
"God, I know now!"

Ari woke up the next day extremely refreshed. This was her first time actually feeling free and she was soaking it all up. Freedom felt good. She sent out a mass text to Evey and Mischa to let them know she was doing really well and was excited to come home later this evening. They'd respected her wishes to not correspond with her during her trip so that she could stay focused on the reason she came to Atlanta in the first place. She did admit she missed her girlfriends so a sweet message to remind them that she loved them and appreciated them didn't interfere with her focus. They both responded with their usual displays of affection igniting Ari's childlike excitement to be reunited with her soul sisters.

Last night, after listening to the same kind of worship music Dr. Sinclair introduced her to, she prayed and got inspiration from God on the direction for the letters she had to write to her parents. Surprisingly, the letter to her mother was easy. It was her father's letter that she struggled with.

She knew nothing about the man other than his love for classical music and pianos. She pressed through the struggle and wrote the letter anyhow. She accepted the medicinal aspect of this assignment and assumed that was the reason Dr. Sinclair instructed her to do this. If she would have to read the letters aloud to him, that would be another hurdle.

Since today was her last day in Atlanta, she made plans to go shopping at Lenox Square Mall, but not before feeding her face. She was starving. Once she showered, she dressed herself in an olive green romper and a light blue denim crop jacket.

She then conditioned her hair to tackle the frizz so that her curls would be a little more tamed. She placed a white oleander clip in her hair and headed out to go have breakfast.

She took herself to Sway, a modern restaurant inside the Hyatt Regency Hotel where she stayed. After stuffing herself with strawberry and crème oatmeal, eggs and fresh baked biscuits, she headed to Lenox Square Mall, which would be the highlight of her day. The first store she would go to was Aldo, for shoes.

She waltzed down aisles with no particular shoe in mind. She waited for something to catch her eye. A strappy pair of high-heeled sandals caught her attention. They were blue with flower prints. She reached for them and put one on.

"Oh my God, I love those! They're so cute on you," a woman said.

Ari grinned and turned her foot inward. Admiring the shoe.

"You think they're cute?" Ari asked.

"Yes, you should get 'em. Treat yourself girl," the woman encouraged.

Ari looked at the woman and realized she was the beauty on Dr. Sinclair's photo- his fiancée. She covered her mouth simply astounded at such a chance encounter.

"Is your fiancé Dr. Sinclair the Christian therapist?"

The woman blushed like a high-school teenager.

"Yes. How do you know him? Are you one of his clients?"

Suddenly Ari was pummeled by shame. Her smile was tapered just a little. She was embarrassed to admit that the way in which she knew this woman's future husband was through his therapy sessions. *I'm a quack!* She figured this lady had every right to be apprehensive and unfriendly.

"Yeah. I'm his client. I was referred to him by a friend and encouraged by my pastor to come down here. I'm actually from Chicago." Ari surmised that this unsolicited information about herself would soften the blow from the reality of who she really was.

"Aw, really? That's so brave of you to come fly out here to seek Christian therapy aside from your pastor's counsel. I think it's always admirable when women, especially, take that leap of faith to become spiritually and mentally healthy. And girl you're good, because I hate planes." She waved her hands gesturing her distaste for flying.

She took that same hand and shook Ari's hand. Ari felt a warm sense of relief. This woman didn't at all give Ari the impression that she thought she was a psychopath or a straightjacket candidate.

"My name is Naomi. I'm sure my honey bunches of oats probably told you that already," she said fluttering her eyelashes girlishly.

"Yeah. He did. He's so blessed to have someone like you to walk with him through life."

"And I'm just as blessed. I can't wait to spend the rest of my life with that man! He's a diamond in my heart."

Ari noticed that the same awestruck gaze Dr. Sinclair had when he thought of Naomi was the same expression Naomi had when she thought of him. It was a charming thing to witness.

"So, are you going to get those Jessica Simpson's or not? Because I think I want them! And they're on sale!"

Ari was tickled by Naomi's free spirit.

***

"You seem upbeat. That homework assignment must have been more therapeutic than I thought. Should I ask you how you're doing?" Dr. Sinclair asked.

Ari felt like she was floating on a cloud when she walked into his office. Shoe shopping with his fiancée boosted her confidence. She was a joy to be around. Dr. Sinclair was really marrying a gem.

"I'm fantastic Dr. Sinclair! You want to know what I did today?" She asked him. She felt like a little kid about to tell her father something that he'd be proud to hear.

"Sure! Have a seat. Make yourself at home," he said happily. He folded his hands on the table and gave her his undivided attention.

"I went to Sway for breakfast and I stuffed myself," Ari told him.

"Ok."

For some reason his attentiveness made her even happier.

"I needed to burn off that food, so I decided to go to Lenox Mall and I went to Aldo to get some shoes. And guess who I ran into? This is so funny! You're going to laugh when you hear this!"

Dr. Sinclair chuckled.

"I ran into your amazing fiancée, Naomi!"

"Oh, really?" He asked.

"Yes! Oh my God! I thought, what a coincidence. We talked for a little while. Dr. Sinclair, she's so nice and her spirit is the sweetest. I just love her and I barely know her. I see why you adore her so much. She's an angel."

Ari caught herself staring into that place where love was the head of state and supremely unimpeded. Maybe that's where the two of them met whenever they thought of each other. Maybe this was the love God was trying to show her she could have all along. What a cunning way to reveal it.

"Dr. Sinclair, God is so breathtakingly awesome. I know now! He just showed me the love I never knew I could have. It's agape! You know, what you were telling me about yesterday? The love he'd been trying to give me for so long. God, I know now!"

Ari wiped away her tears of joy and giggled. Dr. Sinclair smiled and rose from his seat.

"You want some peach tea?" He asked.

QUEEN ARI
"And as the wind continued to blow, she opened her eyes…"

August

"You can't be healed of anything that you are afraid of or refuse to open up about. The first step to deliverance is admittance-admitting that you even have a problem. The second step is confronting the problem. Confronting the problem means you recognize and understand that this issue needs to be dealt with now and not later. Depending on the circumstances, deliverance may not happen overnight. But, it can happen when you start admitting that an issue exists within you and stop focusing on your neighbor's problems. Your problem or problems are uniquely attached to you and you only. Be delivered! Get free! Deliverance is the children's bread!"

"Amen," Ari said in unison with the rest of the people from her church.

Months had passed since her eye opening therapy sessions with Dr. Sinclair in Atlanta. Unfortunately, she hadn't gotten too far. It was true that she was ready to be set free from any lingering demon she'd become all too familiar with, but her problem was bigger than that now. Identifying the how, as in "how will I do this?" is what bogged her down and occasionally even caused her to place the idea of receiving complete deliverance on the back burner. She did accept one thing though: she would have to go on a quest to find her mother first. Once she found her mother, she could find her father.

This sounded so simple. The information she'd gathered about her mother's whereabouts, however, sent her on a wild goose chase that led to nowhere. All of her efforts to reconcile her past seemed futile. The choir began to sing as the congregation was invited to the altar to receive prayer.

"I will never be, bound again. I've got my liberty. I'm finally free," the choir crooned.

"Do you want to go up for prayer Ari?" Evey asked.

Ari shook her head in agreement as tears of mostly frustration rolled down her amber cheeks. Mischa, who sat next to her, grabbed her hand to go with her as well. The three ladies stood in line until they reached their pastor. Ari held her head down. He knew her story very well and even assisted in her efforts to find her mother. For some reason, however, she felt abashed. She'd gone to another state to seek counsel, even spent some time away from the church, and still was back at square one.

"Hold your head up, Daughter," he said.

Ari lifted her head as he rubbed oil on her forehead in the shape of a cross. He put his right hand on her head, left on her chest, and prayed,

"Father God, we come to you as humbly as we know how. I lift up your daughter right now, God. Give her the grace she needs to step out on faith and receive deliverance from the chains of her past. Take hold of her heart and protect her as she walks through the valley of the shadow of death. Cover her mind so that she can keep it stayed on you. Help her to seek you first in all she does, so that she remains steadfast in your presence. So that she will receive the desires of her heart."

"Show her the pathway of life where she can experience your presence in full and partake in the pleasures that sit at your right hand. She freely gives this heavy burden to you. Give her the clarity that she needs. Be her answers. Set fire in all the rooms where the demons of her past have become comfortable. Make it impossible for them to come back by covering the walls with the blood of the lamb and give her back her peace God. Give her rest in Jesus' name. Amen."

Ari exhaled slowly and wiped her face dry. *Okay, God. I'm going to leave all of my troubles here at the altar. I trust you, Lord. I know that you will give me what I need to conquer this mountain. It's all in your hands now, Father.* Everything that she couldn't control would have to die at the altar, including her old self.

***

"You make me happy. You make me whole. You take the pain away. I'm so in love with you."

The voice of gospel singer Tasha Cobbs chimed through Ari's headphones as she lay under a tree at Lake Michigan. The sun expressed its allure across the sky and the breeze from the lake was blissful. Church service this past Sunday had given her all the credence she needed to fully enjoy this Wednesday afternoon. God had been so good to her thus far, and she held onto her faith that He would continue to be so. She stretched out on the blanket she'd brought with her and closed her eyes.

One of her favorite scriptures, Colossians 3:2 came to mind, "Think about the things of heaven and not the things on earth."

Ari let her mind travel to places she believed resembled heaven. No more pain. No more crying. No more stressing about the things that didn't belong in her hands in the first place. The wind from the lake was God's blanket of peace spreading over her. A sweet fragrance came with it. And as the wind continued to blow, she opened her eyes to find a man sitting next to her.

She stretched, and then cordially glanced over at the man once she caught a full view of him. He was very appealing to look at with his short wavy hair, brown skin, and sculpted goatee that accented his strong jaw-line. It was his milky brown eyes that actually caught her observation; they seemed to be shrouded with melancholy. She took her ear buds out of her ears and sat up, folding both legs underneath her body. Oddly, the man didn't make her feel uneasy. She smiled at him once more and then looked toward the lake. The wind blew her thick curly black mane, causing it to temporarily blur her vision. She grabbed a hairpin adorned with rhinestones from her bag and pinned the front portions of her hair back to keep it out of her face.

Her voice was calm, "Isn't the lake beautiful? I love watching it from here."

The man didn't respond but stared at the water. Ari looked over and extended her hand to him. "My name is Ari. Ari Tamar Hughes." Sharing her entire government name with confidence.

She shook his hand energetically as he spoke, "Noah. Noah Elijah L'rieux."

"It's nice to meet you, Noah. Hey, would you like some of my pineapples? They're very fresh," she told him as she pulled the container out of her lunch bag and handed it to Noah with a fork. She watched as he speared a pineapple ring and bit into the juicy fruit.

"You can have them if you want," she offered. "I've eaten enough."

"Thank you," Noah said, going for another one.

He seemed peculiar, somewhat estranged. "Are you from Chicago?" She asked.

"No, I'm from Georgia. I actually just moved up here this past weekend."

"Really? That's great! You're going to love Chicago. I don't know about our weather, but for the most part you will enjoy this beautiful city."

"I saw a few things downtown today. I took some pictures too." He took out his phone and showed her the sights he'd captured. Ari commented, "Nice, nice," as he flipped from one snapshot to the next.

Ari was feeling more and more comfortable around this perfect visitor. His company was lovable.

"Do you have any family and friends here?" She asked.

"No, I have a sister in Georgia who might move up here soon, her and her … fiancé.

A short pause crept in. Ari took that as her cue to continue the conversation by sharing more information about herself.

"I don't have that much family either. I'm an only child. A lot of the people I've met over the years have become my family though. Oh and I can't forget God. He's been everything to me."

"What about your parents? Are you not close with them?" He asked.

That question sort of caught her off guard and stung a little. But, to talk about her parents with someone who knew nothing about her or her life would be liberating.

"Not really. I never knew my dad. He left when I was young. My mom resented me because of him. I put up with her until I went to college. She said and did a lot of things to me that affect me to this day." Ari paused and squinted as she pushed loose strands of hair out of her face.

"There was one time she told me I was ugly because I had my daddy's face. I locked myself in the bathroom, crying and staring at my reflection. I always thought I looked like my mom; she's absolutely gorgeous. But when she told me that, it hurt me to the core. I didn't know what my daddy looked like and I kept trying to see what she saw." Ari kept her eyes on the lake.

A tear seeped from her eye. This felt easy actually sharing her testimony. Maybe her willingness to share her story would make him feel free enough to share his. But he didn't. They continued to talk, but about lighter subjects, like the summer activities in the city. She told him about some of the festivities he'd just missed, including the Taste of Chicago and Lollapalooza, both held in Grant Park.

Ari didn't want to cut off this fellowship but she had to go to Bible study in another hour. She told him she was about to head home. "Hey," she said to Noah while packing up her belongings. "You know, the temperature will drop soon. Are you going to stay out here?"

"Um, no. I'm going to leave too." He told her.

"Oh, then do you care to walk me home? I live right over there." She pointed up the street.

"Gladly," Noah answered before rising to his feet.

The walk was peaceful. At the door of her building, Ari stopped and faced Noah. His eyes were piercing with interest, but she could feel the sadness in them communing with her own unhappiness. If time had permitted, she would have talked with him a little longer.

"Thanks for walking me home, Noah," Ari said and smiled.

"Oh no problem," he replied.

"So I guess I'll see you around sometime," Ari said.

"Um, yeah."

The delicate silence blocked their chemistry. Ari was expecting him to ask for her number, just as many men before him did. But he didn't ask and she dared not ask for his.

"Well alright then. Goodnight, Mr. L'rieux." She smiled before walking into her building.

She went upstairs and into her second floor apartment.

"Now that was a mysterious but nice encounter. I'm probably never going to see that man again."

QUEEN ARI
"... this was the dragon ..."

"Maybe you should hire a private investigator, Ari," Evey spoke before she took a spoonful of frozen yogurt in her mouth.

"I think you should too, Ari. It would get rid of some of this stress and save you from going on blank missions. Hey, I heard that some retired police officers become private investigators. I can ask Prentice if any of his police friends do that type of work," Mischa told her.

The three women sat outside of Z. Berry's, a frozen yogurt shop in Hyde Park Plaza enjoying a less humid day. Ari thought about the idea of hiring a private investigator while she watched a mother pushing her baby in a stroller and a toddler walking beside her.

"I don't know, y'all. It sounds like a good idea, but I don't want to be a stalker or anything. My thing is this: maybe the reason I'm having such a hard time finding my mother is because she doesn't want to be found. To be honest, I'm starting not to really care. I think I just want to put this to rest."

"Ari, you're not being a stalker when you're trying to heal. Nothing is wrong with attempting to find the woman who gave birth to you. Yes, I know she caused you a lot of pain, but she is your mother. You need answers. You need freedom. You're not completely free, Ari. Your heart is being attacked by unforgiveness, pain, rejection, and abandonment. You can't keep operating like this! I want to see my friend whole, healthy, and happy. I don't see this as being a stalker unless you mean that you're stalking healing and liberty," Evey said emphatically.

163

There's nothing like the sting of tough love. It actually felt better than all the years of experiencing the effects attributed to the lesser forms of love. She needed to admit that her unwillingness to push harder for healing stemmed from her fear of confronting the monsters that had a death grip on her heart. And she needed to admit she was tired of fighting. Tired of fighting complacency and tired of trying to protect the unhealthy, dysfunctional portions of her life.

"You're right. I guess it's time for me to stop making excuses and truly pursue this. How soon can Prentice find me a private investigator?"

***

Ari's phone rang softly underneath her as she slept on her couch in the living room. Rain thumped heavily against her windows. She reached for her phone and answered it.

"Hello?"

"Good evening, may I speak to Ari Hughes please?"

"This is she," she responded, sitting upright.

"This is Gregory Hill, the private investigator you hired," the man on the other end of her phone said.

Ari's heart punched her in the chest without warning. Did this man find her mother? He had to or else why would he be calling? She'd just spoken with him a few days ago after Mischa's husband, Prentice, introduced them. She really wasn't expecting him to call her back so soon. To be honest, she was hoping he didn't which is why she hadn't saved his number.

"Yes," she said apprehensively.

"I found your mother. She currently lives alone in Rogers Park. Would you---"

"How sure are you about that? Did you see her? Does she look like any of the pictures I gave you," Ari cut him off with her breathless inquiries.

"I'm very positive I've located your mother, Ms. Hughes. I can take you to her if you'd like," he offered.

"No, that's okay," Ari declined.

She wasn't sure she was ready to see her mother today. She wanted to sedate her emotions and rearrange her thoughts first.

"I can email you her whereabouts and the photos I took of her coming out of her home, and going to various places in the city upon payment for completing my assignment," he told her.

"Ok that's fine. My email is ari_thughes@gmail.com. Thank you," Ari said before hanging up the call.

Is this really happening? My God, after all these years, I've actually found her? What am I supposed to do now? Her mind was running a hundred miles per hour. She could barely allow herself to make the payment online to this private investigator. An inner war instigated a debate between wanting to know and not wanting to know; she couldn't decide what was best. It's as if God ceased this agitation because she unexpectedly received a picture text from the private investigator at that moment. With trembling hands, Ari clicked the button on her phone to open the picture. It seemed to take longer than usual for it to load for full view. A picture of a woman walking down the porch steps of her house with a cigarette in between her fingers displayed on the screen of Ari's phone. Nothing could refute the truth: this was the dragon, also known as- her mother.

Ari locked the screen and slid her phone across the table as if it was suddenly covered in slime. She quickly made the payment to Mr. Hill and closed her laptop. She didn't want to wait to receive the rest of the photos or information regarding where her mother could be found. She jumped up from the couch and pulled her colorful rain boots and umbrella out of the closet before going outside to face the rain.

The trek to Starbucks through the puddles of water and onslaught of rain reminded her of her own life. No matter where she went, the puddles of water either caused her to make a short detour or to hop over them to avoid getting her feet wet. Receiving this new, extremely reliable information was a puddle of a different caliber. It was too big of a puddle to jump over and too much trouble to find another route; she had to step in it and allow herself to get wet. She rushed into the café only to run into the handsome stranger she'd met at the lake a few days ago.

"Hey, Ari," he managed to say.

"Oh! Hi, Noah! It's nice to see you. So um, about our weather …" She laughed infectiously and he couldn't help but laugh with her.

She walked over to the table he was at and sat in the seat adjacent to his. He stared at her intently, as if he were admiring her natural beauty. *Why is he looking at me like that? Maybe this was a bad idea. He never even asked for my number. Maybe I should just leave. Who told me to sit here anyway?* Ari started to look around the room to avoid making eye contact with Noah.

Her hair was styled into a single French braid and it, along with the multi-colored scarf that served as her headband, was soaking wet. The undivided attention he gave caused her to constantly push the free strands of her hair behind her ears.

"Why does your jewelry always blind me?" He jokingly asked.

Ari gave him a smile that was mixed with a hint of confusion.

Noah chuckled, "Yeah. Last week your pendant reflected the light and almost blinded me. Now it's your earrings."

"Oh," she laughed, "I'm sorry." She pinched the pendant that had long since replaced the one her first love had given her years ago. She'd actually left it at his tombstone on the anniversary of his death last year.

"Were you coming for coffee? I'll get it for you- my treat," he rendered.

"Oh, no. For some reason, I had this craving for these Mandarin cakes they sell."

He smiled at her and she blushed.

"My sister loves those things." He excused himself and bought her two packs of the seashell shaped pound cakes. When he came back to their table, he placed them in her hand. She was flattered by this gesture. She smirked when she looked at the actual name of the cakes. They were called *Madeleines* not *Mandarin*s yet he knew what she was talking about.

The two stayed in Starbucks until it closed three hours later. Ari felt so relaxed talking, mainly because it allowed her to keep her mind off her woes. The conversation sparked gleefulness within her. She was elated he offered to walk her home again.

167

Ari told Noah about her profession as a curator at her own art gallery in Bronzeville, and he listened with interest. She was even more pleased when he told her he'd come by to see it. An opportunity to exchange numbers with him perfectly presented itself.

"So, I guess this is it for today," she turned around and said.

"Yeah. I enjoyed myself with you," he said sincerely. She could sense he was becoming more uninhibited and less guarded.

"I did as well," she told him.

Noah blushed as she reached for a hug. She had to stand on her toes, and they both laughed at her attempt to do so. His embrace was warm and friendly.

"Well okay, I'll talk to you tomorrow then. Let's hope it doesn't rain," she laughed.

"I know, right? Then I'd have to find some polka dot rain boots like yours."

"Oh no, please don't do that." Ari continued laughing.

"Goodnight, Ari," he said smiling.

Ari eagerly skipped up the stairs to her apartment. She'd purposely placed a velvet rope around her lifestyle after a string of unsuccessful relationships, including the one with Carter, the married man. She realized that in order for her to enter into a fruitful relationship with anyone, she'd first have to resolve her "daddy issues". Running into Noah again ignited the fervor to complete the task of tying up those loose ends with her mother so she could finally find her father. Although it was late, she planned to take the ride to Rogers Park and see her mother tonight.

Upon walking into her home, she let out a startled scream!

There was someone lying on her couch! She hurriedly flipped on the switch near her front door and shouted, "Who's there?"

Before she could say anything else, she realized exactly who it was- Mischa. Her face was soaked with tears and Ari knew that her unannounced visit meant that something was seriously wrong. She ran over to her crying friend and discovered a busted nose and black eye.

Ari's eyes protruded from their sockets as she wrapped Mischa into a warm hold Sadly, she wasn't surprised though. Prentice couldn't handle his liquor; every time he drank, he would turn into a sadistic, manipulative man and abusive towards his wife. *Guess I'll have to visit my mother another day.*

QUEEN ARI
"Fragile glass hearts are no match for steel toe fury."

"So what happened, Mischa?" Ari asked.

It was now morning and the two of them had rested tranquilly as could be expected. When Ari discovered her friend in her home the night before obviously beaten, she didn't say anything. She instead grabbed a blanket and pillow to make her feel unworried, cleaned her face up, and gave her two Tylenol PM painkillers so she wouldn't have to cry herself to sleep. Because this situation had transpired a few times before, all of this was a routine for Ari. Mischa sniffed and attempted to wipe away her falling tears.

"I swear, Ari, he hadn't put his hands on me in weeks since we've been seeing a therapist. I don't know what else to do. It's like he gambles a lot and takes his anger out on me when he loses!" Mischa dropped her head and wiped her cheeks as the tears continued to fall. A few minutes of stillness that echoed feelings of heartache and shame passed, then she said, "I know what you're thinking and you're probably right. I just don't want to get a divorce, Ari. I love him. I just wish he wouldn't hurt me like this."

Ari's insides rattled with displeasure. She hated abuse, mainly because she knew what it felt like to be behind the hands of it. Prentice had broken one of Mischa's arms and two ribs on separate occasions. Their marriage was not only changing Mischa physically; it was transforming her psychologically too. Ari noticed that the bubbly, vivacious girl she met in college had become extremely insecure and somewhat lifeless. Prentice had literally been beating the life out of this woman.

Ari looked at her friend and wept for her despair. *Oh, God! This can't be your plan. I don't care how much she loves him. It's time for her to end this and this time it needs to be for good!* Ari feared that if Mischa stayed any longer with that dreadlocked monster, he would probably kill her. Fragile glass hearts are no match for steel toe fury.

"Mischa, how long are you going to accept this abuse? You don't deserve this! This isn't love. A woman should never have to trade abuse for love! He doesn't love you if he can put his hands on you like he's done so many times. God said that men should love their wives as they love their own bodies. Well, Prentice drinks alcohol like it's water that should tell you he doesn't even love his own body. You were meant to be his helpmeet not his punching bag. You are worth so much more than what he's giving you. I can't stand seeing you like this. You have to get out now, Mischa."

Mischa nodded her head but Ari could tell that she wasn't completely convinced. How close to the grave would her husband have to take her in order for her to wake up? The sudden ringing of Ari's phone broke the quietude between them. She ran into her bedroom to catch the call before she'd missed it.

"Good morning," a male voice on the other end spoke.

Ari gushed and her insides melted. It was Noah.

"Hey, Love. How are you?" She asked him as she sat on the bed.

"I'm good. I thought about you when I woke up, so I wanted to call and talk to you for a while if that's ok," he invited.

His mellow mood subdued her nerves. She fiddled with her hair as she continued to talk.

"So you called me as soon as you woke up? That's heartwarming," she told him.

"Yup I sure did. I didn't even brush my teeth. Breath stank and everything. Can you smell it?" He playfully asked before blowing into the phone.

Ari cackled loudly. Suddenly, her front door slammed and she jumped at the sound. Ari got up from her bed and walked into the living room only to find an empty space. Mischa left and didn't even bother to say goodbye. Ari shook her head and went back into her bedroom. There was no use in trying to call her and asking her to come back. Mischa was just one of those people with a one-track mind governed by stubbornness.

Ari was fully engaged in her conversation with Noah until she went to her art gallery. She couldn't help but admit he was a peaceful distraction since her life was chaotic and lonely. Although Noah was a newcomer, she couldn't help but sense they had more in common than what had yet to be revealed. He was hiding some things, probably buried pain, but she couldn't focus on that too much until she unburied hers.

Later that evening, she made it her mission to drive to Rogers Park. Sitting outside the address of her mother's, a flash flood of old memories rushed her mind: the constant beatings, the ridicule, the lack of love and support a daughter needed from a mother, the tears, and nights of going to bed on an empty stomach as a method of punishment for rebellion. All of it provoked her to cry until her chest hurt.

She reached into the glove compartment and pulled out the letter she wrote to her mother per Dr. Sinclair's assignment during her last session with him. He didn't require her to read either letters to him. She just had to write them. He told her that the letters would assist in unlocking the door of unforgiveness. She read it aloud,

"Dear Momma, you may not believe me but I love you. I love you because you brought me into this world. Your hate towards me taught me unconditional love. The anger you used on me taught me how to look for happiness. I don't ever remember seeing you smile at me, so I learned how to smile at others. The resentment you showed me helped me to appreciate life and all that I'm capable of. How you treated me doesn't control me anymore. All of those mean words you threw at me, they are no longer stuck on me. I pulled them off and now I love who I am. I love my reflection even though I'm a carbon copy of you. Sincerely your daughter, Ari Tamar Hughes."

Her soft sobs were hushed when the headlights of a car flashed in the rearview mirror. The car parked right behind hers and a person casually exited the driver's seat. The alarm sounded and the person walked to the house, Ari now knew belonged to her mother. The person was indeed the woman she had driven to Rogers Park to see. Ari imagined herself jumping out of the car and running up to her screaming, "Momma! Momma! It's me, your daughter! Did you miss me?"

And she imagined her mom would respond, "Yes, Ari, my angel. I did miss you. I'm so happy to see you! Listen, my sweet daughter, I have to tell you something: I'm so sorry for hurting you."

"I'm so sorry for what I put you through. I was young when I had you and still trying to get my life together. I took everything out on you and you really didn't deserve any of it. Please forgive me, Sweetie."

The house door slamming pulled her out of her imagination and back into reality. Past images of abuse came back and bullied her into staying in the car. And sadly, she did just that.

QUEEN ARI
"So what is 'The Passion'?"

In an effort to take her mind off of the disappointment she felt, she had decided to share the details of last night's experience with Noah. *I still can't believe I didn't get out of the car! Like seriously, Ari? After driving all the way to the other side of town, you were too afraid to get out of the car and speak to her? This is all so aggravating!* Her thoughts were becoming so overwhelming that she felt like she was suffocating. She had purposely been avoiding the subject with Noah because it was difficult to discuss openly, but Ari realized that talking to him would serve as a much needed antidepressant.

Today, she would finally get to see him again as he agreed to stop by her art gallery. It was a beautiful breezy day in Chicago, and Ari decided to ride her bike to work because the scenic views of the city along with the nice weather always provided her with comfort. Her shop was nestled in a shady spot on 31st Place, right off of Pershing Road, and looked quite inviting from the outside. On the inner part of the large window that faced the street sat a large arrangement of brightly colored orange carnations. Orange had been Ari's favorite color since her high school prom, and it would forever remain as such.

Her attempts to remain busy in an effort to tranquilize the butterflies with annoying wings failed. She couldn't fool herself any longer. She really couldn't wait to see Noah.

"I can't believe, you've met somebody, Ari! You're finally letting your guards down. I wish he would get here already! He must be something for you to have pressed out them kinky curls," Evey poked fun.

"Shut up," Ari laughed.

Ari hoped he would feel welcomed by the vanilla and pumpkin aromas and would be intrigued by the vibrant African American art and sculptures on the walls. Jill Scott's voice singing, "The Fact Is I Need You," crooned through the radio speakers just as the gallery's front door chimed in acknowledgement of someone's entrance. Her hands felt like she'd been playing in water all day, as they were soaked in her perspiration.

"Is that him?" Evey eagerly asked.

Ari gasped and ran upstairs to catch her bearings. She stood nearby the staircase and listened as Evey greeted someone, possibly Noah.

"Hello. Welcome to Ari's Art Studio. If you're looking for anything in particular, just let me know."

A brief pause went by and she heard his voice, "Um, well as a matter of fact I am 'looking for something in particular'. I'm looking for Ari." Noah smirked.

"Oh … um, ok. Hold on one second, "she heard Evey say.

Evey's footsteps echoed up the stairs as she rushed to announce the arrival of Ari's friend. As she tried to calm her nerves, Ari gave herself a much needed pep talk, "This is it! He's actually here. It's time to go down and see him, Ari. We got this. No need to be nervous."

"Oh, my God! He is gorgeous!! Where did you find him, Ari? Wait, why are you hiding up here! Come on girl and say hi to your boo," Evey goofed.

"He's not my boo! He's just a friend, Evey," Ari said while blushing.

"Oh hush, whatever. He ain't gone be a *friend* for long!"

They both walked down the stairs to greet Noah. He stood up and watched as the two women approached him. His bright thousand-watt smile warmed Ari's heart. Her ebony hair was bone straight and flowed freely as she met him with a tight embrace. The tantalizing scent of his sweet yet masculine cologne teased her senses as Noah held onto Ari's frame a little tighter and a little longer than she held onto his. It was clear that he did not want to let her go.

"I'm glad you were able to make it. How are you, Love?" She asked him, as she offered a shy smile.

"Never better," he softly responded.

Then Evey cleared her throat, interrupting this gleeful moment. Ari giggled.

"Evey, this is my friend, Noah. Noah, this is my girlfriend, slash business partner, and a wonderful sister in Christ, Miss Evelyn Graceland."

"Pleasure to meet you, Evelyn." Noah gave her a genuine expression and shook her hand.

Evey snapped her head over to Ari. "Look at his *smile*, Girl. You know he's going to be out of the friend zone in no time!" She whispered in between giggles. She poked Ari in her side. Ari's infectious laugh caused Noah and Evey to burst out into laughter, too.

"I can't stand you, Evey!"

"I know, but that will not change how much I love you." Evey blew a kiss at Ari then turned to leave. "I'd better get back to work." Just as she was walking out the door, she stopped in her tracks and turned to face Ari once more. "Oh, how did I forget? I sold *The Passion,* right before you made it in today!" She exclaimed excitedly.

"Really? Who bought one this time?" Ari asked happily.

"A young minister; he cried when he saw it."

"Wow. I wish I was here," Ari replied.

"Come with me, Noah," said Ari before leading him by the hand. "I'm going to take you to the upper room."

Ari and Evey looked at each other and simultaneously broke out into a tune, "In the upper rooooooom," then dissolved into laughter again.

The gaiety caused Noah to shake his head in merriment. He followed Ari up the stairs to a place where the art overstock was kept. It was a massive attic with beautifully painted pictures in all sizes. Each one was categorized and placed neatly in its respective place on shelves.

"So what is *The Passion?*" Noah asked.

"It's my depiction of the crucifixion of Jesus. It's also one of my most popular pieces because it so different from all of the other artists' depictions of it." Ari paused and thought back to where it all began. "*The Passion* is one of my very first paintings. I'm always in awe of how much we've accomplished since then."

Holding her finger up as if it were a compass, she made a clicking noise with her tongue and walked deeper into the room. Then, she stopped at the shelf in front of her and flipped through the tabs.

"Bingo! Okay I got it."

She slid a canvas out and Noah was absolutely awestruck at what his eyes beheld. The painting was 36' by 26' inches with a light orange sky as its background. But what stood out was the style of the painting itself. The cross appeared as if it could be taken right off the canvas, and the way Ari painted Jesus was by far the most unique depiction he'd ever seen. Standing close to the painting, you could see Jesus' body was composed of different hues of whites, pinks, greens, and so on in small dots. The colors meshed together to form a complete picture when standing further away from it; this was a style of art known as Pointillism.

"Wow," Noah exhaled, "this is breathtaking. I've never seen anything like it. What made you do it this way?" Noah kept staring at the painting.

"Well we don't know exactly what race Jesus was so I incorporated every color I could to recreate him for this painting. Depending on where you stand and how far you stand, his color changes. It represents the fluidity of his physical identity."

Noah moved in for a closer examination, and then took several steps back to see the change. "I can't stop looking at it," he said transfixed.

Ari laughed, "I'm glad you like it. I was in so much pain when I made this."

Noah's attention turned to Ari. "Why?"

"I painted this right before I moved out of my mom's house for good. We had gotten into one of many arguments. This one was about me needing money to go away for school."

"She slapped me just because I'd asked, telling me I'd never be anything because of my so-called daddy and school wasn't going to change that. She said a lot of other degrading things that I wish not to ever let come out of my mouth. All I could remember was being deeply hurt and upset. I just wanted to die."

"I cried for hours that night, wondering why my mom hated me so much. Then out of nowhere I saw this image of Jesus in a vision. So I got up, and I began to paint. It took me eight months to finish it. The vision reminded me that I was not alone in my pain," she said thoughtfully, "and that Jesus suffered from the hatred of others too, then ultimately died for everyone—including the ones who hated him. Out of all the paintings I've created over the years, this one will always remain close to my heart."

She looked away, wiping her eyes. Although she was completely at peace, she left out the part about the death of her first love and the full details of that night which inspired this painting, to keep things from getting too deep. She would eventually tell him if ever she was granted the time, but not today. Noah stood still. The unwelcomed silence stirred up doubts in Ari's mind: *Great job, Ari! Now you've made things awkward. He probably doesn't know whether to come over and comfort you or to just stay where he is. Hurry up and get it together, Girl! You're losing him!* She regained her composure and looked at Noah with a huge smile.

"You are a fantastic artist with a great imagination, Ari. It is so obvious that you are anointed for this. I really like what you have accomplished here. My sister has to see this. I mean, wow."

"Thank you so much. I promise I couldn't have done it without God. He's my best friend and inspiration," she said.

She noticed Noah smiled but it only lasted for a moment. *What is he hiding behind those sad eyes?*

"So this is my studio-my baby," she gushed.

"I'm impressed. I really am," he affirmed.

Time slipped away from them and soon Evey was calling up the stairs to let them know that the shop was about to close. She came to the upper room with a mischievous look on her face.

"It was very nice to meet you, Noah. I'm sure I'll see more of you soon," she laughed, trying to dodge a pinch from Ari.

Noah cheerfully responded, "Yeah, I'm sure you will. Well, that's if Ari doesn't mind."

Evey elbowed Ari as she addressed Noah. "Her? Naw she don't mind. Shoot don't nobody else come by here for her. As a matter of fact, she definitely doesn't mind. Ain't that right, Sista Girl?"

Ari playfully leered at Evey and mouthed, "I hate you," to Noah's amusement.

"But seriously, Noah," Ari said, "you are always welcome to come by."

Evey slapped her hands together. "Mission accomplished," she exclaimed.

Noah and Ari grinned and shook their heads at each other. "Toodles," Evey said as she walked toward the door.

"We'd better head out too," Ari suggested to Noah. He walked behind her as they went downstairs. She could feel him watching her every move.

"Is your car parked farther down the street? I can take you to it," Noah said.

"Oh no, I didn't drive. It was too nice for me not to ride my bike today." The grandfather clock against the wall gave a muffled boing, its pendulum slowly swinging back left to right. Ari glanced at it and said, "I've got about a half hour before my bus comes though."

"Ari, you must have been around too many paint fumes or something. We live in the same neighborhood. I can take you home," he said.

"Yeah I know," she bashfully replied. "I just didn't want to impose on any plans you may have this evening." Fidgeting with the cross pendant on her necklace, she thought back to her past relationship with Carter. *He definitely taught me not to assume that a man is available just because he's interested.*

"Nonsense," he said, waiting by the door. "You're coming with me, Ari." The tone of Noah's voice reassured Ari in a way that she never thought were possible. Ari quickly shut the computer down, gathered her belongings, turned the lights off, and locked the door behind them. His gestures were chivalrous as he opened the passenger door of his Jaguar for her. She smiled back and got into the car.

The drive back to Hyde Park wasn't long enough for her. She felt safe with him, yet he seemed so secretive. *I hope he isn't a serial killer!* Ari stole a quick glance at Noah and disapprovingly shook her head at her own thoughts. *Oh well, it's too late now. I should have thought about that before I got in his car! Hopefully he's taking me home.* Her suspicions faded when he stopped in front of her apartment and turned on his hazard lights, since there was nowhere to park.

"Thanks again for coming by to see my art studio, Noah. I'm really glad you came," Ari said.

"Thanks for inviting me," Noah replied with his eyes fixed on her. He tilted his ear toward the radio. It was turned down low, but a few lines of Babyface's song "When Can I See You Again," could be heard. He increased the volume, and let his eyes bounce from Ari to the radio and back to her again. She snickered. He reminded her of a nervous high school boy.

"What are you doing tomorrow?" He asked her.

"I have a church retreat to go to up north. I'll be there for the rest of this week," she told him as she laid her head on the headrest.

She lied. She really was going back to see her mother.

"But I'll be back Friday," she added in an encouraging voice.

Noah hesitated for a moment then spoke, "I want to take you out on a date. Will you call me?"

"I will, Love." She leaned over and gave him a kiss on the cheek before attempting to open the door. But Noah quickly turned on the safety lock. Ari giggled, "You're holding me hostage?"

"I would," he said sheepishly, "but I don't want to go to jail." They laughed together like they were old friends. He turned off the safety lock, got out of the car, and opened the door for her. The two of them walked to her apartment. As he trailed behind her, Ari's mind wandered to the life she lived before she truly valued herself. *Had this been a few years ago, tonight would have certainly been ending differently. First I'd tease him for a little while, a game of cat and mouse, and then we'd end up making love. Not this time though.*

Ari had come to realize that her relationship with God was more important than fulfilling any of her physical desires. If Noah's plan was to stay in her life for longer than a few breaths, he would have to fit into her spiritual union.

Before she went inside her building, Noah grabbed Ari's left hand and gently pressed his lips against it. "See you Friday, right?" He asked, looking down at her with his engaging eyes.

"Yeah, I'll see you Friday for sure. "She gave him a "church hug", being careful not to make too much body contact, and floated up the stairs that led to her apartment. *There is something about that man that makes me feel so at ease,* Ari thought as she closed and locked the door.

She walked into the bathroom and ran a warm bubble bath that was presently narrated by Hillsong United's "Oceans (Where Feet May Fail)".

Loneliness nibbled on her heart. She realized she hadn't talked to God in a while and was desperately in need of a reconnection. As she sat in the tub and released a sigh, she finally admitted a truth that she'd been struggling to accept: *I really can't do this on my own.* She prayed from the part of her heart that still ached.

"God, I need you. I need you so badly. Fighting hurts. Not fighting hurts. Sometimes I want to give up. Other times I don't. I feel like I'm going in circles. My happiness never lasts longer than my sadness. Where are you, God? Are you absent because I haven't included you in all of my decisions?"

"Forgive me for going at this the wrong way. I need help. I need your support. Come help me, God. I just want to be happy and free like everyone else. My life has been so unfair. Your Word mentions you are a God of justice. Vindicate me!"

As far as Ari could recall, this was one of the most desperate prayers she'd ever made to God. When she first gave her life to Christ, she told herself she would never be one of those believers who would only go to God when in need. This was different though. She wasn't really looking for Him to fix anything but to give her comfort as He gave her instructions on how to fix it herself. More than anything else, Ari just wanted to know God was there during the sensitive moments in which she felt alone. This is where she would invest her strength to keep moving.

She got out of the tub and dried herself. Once the water drained, she walked into her room and stepped into a satin chemise.

She climbed into her sleigh bed, reached over to her dresser to get her Bible, but it slipped out of her hand. Annoyed, Ari smacked her lips and rolled onto the floor to pick up the now opened Bible. She saw that Psalm 147:3-5 was circled and read the words aloud:

'He heals the brokenhearted and binds up their wounds. He determines the number of the stars and calls them each by name. Great is our Lord and mighty in power; his understanding has no limit."

She didn't remember when she marked that scripture but it sure was on time tonight. Ari felt reassured that God was indeed with her. She smiled, returned the Bible to its rightful place beside her bed, and went to sleep.

QUEEN ARI
"…it is well, with my soul."

Today felt like she was going on her high school prom again. She was preparing for her date with Noah, but her mind drifted to yesterday's events. After leaving the church retreat, she made her second trip to her mother's house only to be met with disappointment. She'd either just missed her or her mother moved because she never came home that night. *I'm starting to feel like there is a reason why I can't see her. What if God is protecting me from her? What if she doesn't want to see me?* Feelings of rejection leaked through the memories of the previous day, but she refused to allow them to dampen her mood.

Ari smoothed out unwanted creases in her strapless tangerine colored knee length dress. It was flowy and carelessly danced in the light air that whooshed through her bedroom window. She accessorized with a pair of gold peep-toe heels and earrings to match. Her buttery-yellow skin had a sun kissed hue perfectly meshing with her dress.

Ring! Ring!

Once again, those pesky butterflies returned as she pressed the intercom,
"Yes?"
"Hello, Ari. This is Noah."
"Okay. I'll be down in a minute."
She walked downstairs and saw Noah standing with his back toward the door. He had flowers in his hands. She opened the door and stepped outside.

Nervously pulling her black straightened hair to one side, Ari looked down at the bouquet and asked, "Are those for me?"

"Yeah, they're for you. You look amazing, Ari."

"Thank you. You don't look half bad either," she replied.

Noah smirked and handed Ari the flowers before they left in his car. Within thirty minutes, the couple was in the Gold Coast area of Chicago, walking arm in arm into the Signature Room, a restaurant on the ninety-fifth floor of the John Hancock building. Noah had reserved a table with a view of both the lake and the north side of the city. They were just in time to see the sun retire into the horizon.

"Oh my God, this is a beautiful view. How did you know about this, Mr. Atlanta native?" She teased.

"Google has become my new BFF," he joked.

Ari laughed loudly then covered her mouth out of embarrassment. Noah chuckled.

"So, how was the church retreat?" He asked.

"It was fantastic! I learned so much." As she began to give him a few highlights, a waiter greeted them while pouring a light green liquid into their wine glasses. Ari looked at the waiter and politely asked, "What is this?"

"Oh, it's our green grape Moscato- one of the specials this evening."

"Thank you," she said.

"You are welcome, Ma'am. I'll be back shortly to take your orders," the waiter responded. He respectfully nodded his head toward Noah. Ari took a sip of her drink.

"How is it? It's not too strong is it?" Noah asked with concern.

"Oh, no it's just fine. Thank you for asking." She stopped before beginning her next sentence.

"So tell me something. It seems like you know more about me than I do about you. You're so mysterious. What are you hiding?" She was going to crack this walnut shell he called home if it was second to the last thing she'd do.

Noah gave her an affectedly coquettish look and stalled. He looked away from her for a minute then back again.

"Okay, Miss Hughes, what would you like to know?"

Ari wanted to know what defined his character, but decided to start off lightly because she didn't want him to tense up.

"I don't know. Tell me the basics. Ummmm … like … when is your birthday?"

"November nineteenth."

"Mine is September twenty-seventh!" Ari positioned herself more cozily in her seat like a child preparing to watch a favorite cartoon. Noah seemed like he was enjoying their conversation, but she couldn't be too sure. They ordered dinner, and Noah had her total awareness by the time their plates were placed before them. She continued to grill him.

"Basketball or football?"

Noah took a bite of his medium well steak. "Football."

"Football? Really, why?"

"Well my dad …" He took a sip of ice water. "My dad used to play."

"Oh okay. Have you played?"

"Just for fun."

She folded her hands on top of the table and leaned forward, "So what's your pet peeve?"

Noah looked out the window and laughed. "You know what? No one has ever asked me that question before." He wiped his mouth and laid the linen napkin across his lap. "I would have to say it's someone who cracks their knuckles. That drives me crazy."

When he stopped talking, she waved her fork in his direction. "Go ahead, tell me more," she urged.

"Well, one of my frat brothers used to do that and I couldn't stand him. Not because he cracked his knuckles, but because he had the most irritating personality. He was one of those guys who felt he needed to prove his manhood all the time. So one day, I showed him exactly how I felt. All of us inductees were lined up for a meeting and we were forced to listen to another one of his many macho-man speeches. I was beyond tired of his voice, and then he cracked his knuckle! That was it for me. I hit him."

Ari's eyes lit up and she covered her mouth to keep wine from dribbling out as she laughed. "What? You hit him?"

Noah seemed to enjoy that she was entertained. "Yes," he managed to say in between laughs. "I hit him so hard I had to crack my own knuckles afterwards."

They both burst out into laughter. *Wow! I honestly can't get enough of him,* Ari thought. She kept it coming with the questions about his likes and dislikes, life experiences, and embarrassing moments. The more they talked, the more comfortable Ari felt in Noah's presence. She described the time she prompted a debate with her high school science teacher about her belief that penguins could fly. Noah leaned back in his chair and smiled.

"I have to go to the bathroom," he told her. "You're making me laugh too hard." He rose and excused himself.

Ari looked out the window to marvel at the beauty of the Chicago streets from where they were. The streetlights and lights from the buildings looked like candles. This day couldn't get any better. As a matter of fact, she didn't want it to end. A waiter came by and offered to pour her more wine from a different bottle. She really wasn't interested in drinking anything else though, so she politely declined. *I don't want to drink too much tonight. Wait? Could that be his intention? Is he trying to get me drunk?*

She suddenly was turned off. Her brow furrowed, and she thought about what she would say to Noah when he returned. As if he heard his name, Noah suddenly appeared and pulled their waiter aside. His face was angry as he spoke, and it was clear to Ari that there was a problem. *Does he know that I refused the wine? Oh my God, is he upset about it? What is going on here?* She couldn't make out what they were saying. The waiter pointed behind her and Ari turned to follow his gaze. A brown skinned woman with a short haircut sat at the table directly behind theirs, and she wore a devilish grin. Her eyes were locked on Noah, and the way she looked at him unsettled Ari. Apparently, the woman appreciated the attention because she lifted her glass up as if she were giving a toast to Noah.

Noah walked back to Ari and threw two one-hundred-dollar bills on the table. "Don't drink that wine," he ordered.

Ari looked up at him, a little baffled.

"Let's go," he said, wrapping his arm around her as she stood to her feet.

"Are you okay? What happened," she asked.

"Nothing," he said blankly.

A hush grew between them as they rode the elevator to the lobby. While waiting for the valet to bring the car, Ari asked, "Are you sure you're okay Noah? Did I say something wrong?"

Noah looked at her and rubbed his face, shaking his head no.

Once the car arrived, he opened the door for Ari, then got into the driver seat and headed towards Lake Shore Drive. Ari was so confused. *What had just happened? Who was that woman? Was that his wife? Ex-wife? Lord knows I am so tired of men and their X FILES! I mean, I have baggage but at least I don't have any X-files. Oh well, it was fun while it lasted. Or was it?*

When he pulled up to her home. Ari unbuckled her seatbelt obviously upset and yanked the door handle. Noah quickly clicked the button to lock her inside as he'd done before. He turned on the overhead light and gently touched her hand.

"I'm sorry, Ari," he said sincerely.

"About what, Noah? I don't understand. What happened back there?"

"I'm not who you think I am," he whispered.

She looked puzzled. "What do you mean? Have you stolen somebody's identity?"

Noah smirked, "No, I'm just not a good guy, that's all. My past with women ... well, it ... how can I say it?" He searched for the right words. "It isn't pretty, Ari."

"Why do you say that?"

"I've hurt almost every woman I've ever known," he admitted to her.

"Physically?"

"Emotionally."

"Why do you think that is?" She asked with genuine concern.

Finally, that shell is breaking! He has to tell me something or I'm going to part ways with him for good. I can't be hurt by anyone else. Not again. Ari could tell that the subject made him extremely uneasy, but she refused to let him keep her from the truth. He unbuckled his seatbelt and rested his hands on the steering wheel. "I hurt them because I was carrying so much hurt myself."

Ari turned to face him completely. "Why?"

Noah inhaled deeply and exhaled slowly before speaking again. His grip on the steering wheel tightened and he closed his eyes. Tears fell down his face. Ari shifted in her seat. *Oh, God! This man is crying? What do I do now?* She wasn't anticipating this at all. She'd done everything she possibly could to ensure he would be free in her company, and now she felt completely vulnerable. It wasn't his tears that gave her pause; it was the fact that she now knew that he spoke her language.

Ari tenderly wiped her hand along his jaw line, where the first tears still lingered. "You're still hurting. You can talk to me, Noah. Tell me what has hurt you."

Noah loosened his grip on the steering wheel and sank into his seat. "When I was younger, I would hurt girls because I was arrogant, absent minded, and selfish. As I got older it continued but it became more deliberate." He stopped and quickly turned his head towards the window. His voice cracked when he spoke again, "Two years ago, my parents died in a plane crash. They were returning from a trip to Trinidad. It was supposed to be a vacation, but they never made it home."

"I wouldn't wish that kind of thing on my worst enemy. I've been trying so hard to get over it but I can't seem to do that completely. I miss them so much and I blame God for their death." He looked at Ari and dropped his eyes in shame. "Ari, I shouldn't be around you. You talk about how God is your best friend so freely. I don't feel the same way though. I do want that kind of relationship but—"

Noah abruptly unlocked the door, got out of the car, and walked around to Ari's side. When he opened her door, she remained seated but turned her body to face his. She looked up at Noah's solemn face.

Reaching up, Ari pulled him down to her. Noah held his head down and sobbed. She placed his head on her chest and softly cried with him. "You have to let it go, Noah. Give this pain to God. He wants you back more than you know. You may not feel it right now, but all things work together for the good of those who love him. You still love him; I know you do. You're just angry, and that's understandable. It's time to let it go now, Noah. You have to let it go."

Ari rubbed Noah's head gently and hummed a hymn by Horatio Spafford titled, "It is Well". Her pastor and the choir of her church sang it often. She couldn't remember all the words but knew they'd sing, "Whatever my lot, thou has taught me to say, it is well, it is well, with my soul."

Noah cried with no restraint, and she silently cried with him.

QUEEN ARI
"She just wanted to finally be accepted..."

"Thank you for calling the office of Dr. Isaiah S. Sinclair. If this is an emergency, please hang up and dial 911. Our office is now closed. Normal hours of service are Monday through Friday 10a.m. to 6 p.m. Special appointments for Saturdays are only arranged with Dr. Sinclair in person. Please leave a detailed message with your name and number and someone will return your call as promptly as possible. Dr. Sinclair appreciates your business. Have a blessed day."

Ari hung up the call. This was the third time she tried to reach out the Dr. Sinclair, only to hear the same outgoing message. She wanted to see if it were possible for her to have a virtual session with him before she made the ultimate leap of faith by speaking with her mother. *Well, today is the day. No more running. I'm going to talk to my mother no matter what, even if it means sleeping in my car until she gets home. I can't move forward until I truly let go of the past. You can do this, Ari!* The thought of Noah opening up to her last night pulled on her heartstrings. She was shocked but also relieved that he felt safe enough to share his struggles.

After last night, Ari made an internal promise to stick with him as he dealt with his issues if he allowed her to do so. She imagined how good she would feel if she were able to help Noah in the same manner in which Dr. Sinclair helped her. No, she wasn't a therapist, but she was a fighter. The sudden growls of Ari's stomach reminded her that she hadn't eaten yet. *I wonder what he's doing now.* She looked for his number in her call log and called him.

The phone rang once and he answered drowsily, "Hello."

"Oh my God, did I wake you? I'm so sorry," Ari spoke, feeling badly.

"No not at all. You don't have to apologize. Are you okay?"

"Oh yeah, I'm marvelous, Love. I was just calling to see if you wanted to go to Valois for breakfast," she offered.

"Breakfast?" He asked.

"Why of course," she giggled. "I wanted to see you today. Sorry for the short notice."

"That sounds nice. What time?"

"Say in an hour?"

"I'll be there."

She hopped out of bed with glee and pulled a peach dress with an empire waistline out of her closet. She sang, "Freedom," by Eddie James in the shower. Budding flowers of jubilation were sprouting up inside of her and she couldn't be more grateful.

The restaurant they were to meet at was a short walk from her home. The sun was beaming merrily and the wind was friendly. It was a perfect August morning. White butterflies were flying around in the nearby park and people were already out and about. Noah hadn't made it to Valois, a restaurant known to be one of President Obama's favorites, so she waited patiently for him.

"Hello," she said with a happy face when she saw him. He was his usual handsome self, wearing a pair of khaki shorts, a white V-neck t-shirt, and white Cole Hann Air Riders.

"Good morning," he replied.

He met her joyful countenance with his own and walked beside her to the line that led to the open kitchen.

The aromas floating around the quaint yet crowded restaurant tickled Ari's nose and excited her appetite. She was famished! Struggling to suppress her hunger pangs, she looked to Noah for a distraction. *He seems to be a little distracted. I wonder what he's thinking.* She softly cleared her throat.

"Is something wrong, Noah?" She asked.

"Uh, no," he said.

The two walked to the serving area and picked up a tray.

"So did you enjoy the walk?" Ari asked.

"As a matter of fact, I did. Best walk I've ever had actually," he told her.

Noah ordered steak, eggs, hash browns, and homemade biscuits. Ari's meal consisted of an English muffin, a feta cheese omelet, and two turkey patties. With trays of food in hand, they took their seats at a table nestled in a corner that was right in front of the window.

"Let's pray," Ari said, bowing her head and reaching for Noah's hands.

"Heavenly Father, we thank you for waking us up this morning. Thank you for giving us another chance to get it right. We thank you for this beautiful day and for this meal that we are about to receive. We also thank you for new beginnings and fellowship. Bless the hands that cooked this meal, bless the hands we hold, and bless this day with your presence. In Jesus' name we do pray. Amen."

Noah said amen and began to eat. "So what do you have planned for today?"

"Nothing really. I need to go up north for a few hours, but that's it," she said.

"Why? Do you have another retreat to go to?" He asked her.

"No. So, tell me about your plans?" She asked him. This was probably the first time she felt the need to keep something from him.

"Well I don't know. Hadn't really given it too much thought. Maybe we can do something together. When will you be back?"

She honestly didn't know. Her car was stocked with things to assist if she needed to sleep in the car for a night or so.

"Uh, I don't know." She abruptly changed the subject. "How are your sister and brother-in-law doing?"

Noah clenched his teeth and his jawbone twitched. If Ari hadn't been paying attention, she would have missed it. *Oh Lord, what now?*

"They're fine I guess. I haven't talked to them in a few days. I might call them today though. Hopefully they've worked out their issues."

Noah had briefly mentioned during one of their telephone conversations that his sister and her fiancé were having premarital struggles. She assumed that's probably why he seemed somewhat aloof. Once they finished breakfast, they sat and talked for what felt like hours. Ari told him about stories in the Bible that he'd yet to read. The way she told them made it seem like they'd happened to somebody she knew. She made the stories leap out of the text and dance before them. He was fascinated. Then, she read the Songs of Solomon to him, acting out the woman's description of her beloved.

"Wow, I really like that story. The way you tell it makes it feel like I was there too. It seems so much more relevant when you describe it. You know what? You should make your own audio Bible," he suggested.

"It'd be perfect for people who really don't like to read or for those who can't read."

"You think so? Sounds like a great idea." Her eyes twinkled with excitement.

Noah repositioned himself in his seat. Ari surveyed him. *I can't do this. I have to tell him the truth. He deserves to know.*

"Noah," she spoke.

"Yeah," he answered, glancing out the window at people walking past.

"I have something to tell you," she muttered.

Noah shifted his eyes to her. "What's that?"

"I didn't go up north just for the church retreat. I mean, that was the primary reason. But there was something else I needed to do there."

He sat up straight. She arrested his attention again. Yesterday he'd revealed some secrets to her and now it was time for her to do the same. "What else did you go up there to do?" Noah inquired.

"Well, I told you that I moved out of my mom's house when I went to college and I never went back." She took a deep breath and continued. "Well ...I tracked her down. She lives up north in Rogers Park. I went by there, but I was too intimidated to actually go see her. But now, I think I'm ready to do it. I think I'm ready to see my mom."

Noah sat quietly for a short period. He looked out the window again.

"I'll go with you," he suggested.

"No. You don't have to do that. I just wanted to let you know because I could tell you thought I was hiding something. I don't want to start off with secrets and lies, you know."

"But I want to go with you," insisted Noah.

It was Ari's turn to stare out the window. Noah sat quietly across from her and watched as she pondered over his recommendation. *Maybe it's not such a bad idea after all. I mean, who's to say that his presence wouldn't make things easier? I do enjoy his company, and it would be nice not to go alone.* Ari relented and accepted his invitation. He paid for their meals and they left. Rogers Park was roughly a forty-minute drive from Ari's place, but the ride seemed much shorter with Noah by her side. Ari parked in front of a brownstone bungalow. Before she could get out of the car, Noah grabbed her hand. Ari looked at him in bewilderment and was about to question him, but he spoke first.

"I think we should pray, Ari."

He gripped her hand tighter. *Did he say we should pray? I don't feel like praying!* She was anxious and didn't want to sit for too long, knowing fear was lurking somewhere close. *God, what am I thinking? Of course we should pray. Neither of us have been here before, and we definitely need your grace.* The two of them held their heads down and closed their eyes.

"Lord, please cover us as we make our way to Ari's mother's home. Stand in front of us and stand behind us. In Jesus name we pray. Amen."

Noah and Ari walked up to the bungalow and looked at her note to double check that the address matched what she had written. She knocked on the door and then rang the doorbell.

"The mailbox is full, Ari," Noah observed, pulling out mail addressed to Angela Austin. "Do you think she still lives here?"

"Yes, she lives here," Ari said. She was trying to look through the window, but it was difficult to confirm whether or not someone was home.

She rang the doorbell again and knocked twice. The door opened a little. Noah handed Ari the mail.

"Momma, is that you? It's your daughter-Ari. Can I come in?"

Ari pushed the door open and waved for Noah to follow her. A combination of overpowering odors bogarted Ari's nostrils and made her cough. *This is mortifying! I know he smells this too.* Noah followed closely behind her, looking around.

The further they went into the cluttered home, the more the odors of cigarette smoke, cat urine, and mildew reeked. The rotating fan and ceiling fan did nothing but spread the stench. It was evident the person who lived here was a hoarder. Junk was everywhere.

Ari and Noah were startled when a woman walked into what appeared to be the living room, wearing a pair of grey leggings and an oversized navy and green flannel top with the sleeves cut off. Her hair seemed to be the same curly texture as Ari's but had visible strands of grey and was unkempt. It was tied back in a tangled ponytail. The woman sat down in the only available seat in the room, lit a cigarette that she had pulled from her pocket, and took two puffs. Ari searched for any traces of light in those tiny eyes that they shared. To her dismay, there was only menacing darkness in her mother's glare. Life seemed to have taken its toll on Ms. Angela Austin, in a mean way.

"Whatchu want?" The woman said, her cigarette dangling between her lips.

"Momma, I—"

"Don't come up in here with this stranger and think you can call me momma like it's all honky dory. I ain't seen you in years and now you wanna come up in here talkin' 'bout some damn MOMMA? Momma my behind," she spat.

"I tried to come and see you, but you weren't in any of the places that I searched."

"So, what you sayin'? You came here to make me look like the bad guy or something? You got some nerve. I knew you was gon' be just like yo no good daddy, just runnin' off an' leavin' me like I don't exist."

"Momma, I came here to make amends and establish a relationship with you."

"For what? I ain't got no money for you! You Miss Big shot now anyway. Got yo lil business and all. Yeah, I heard about you. You think you somethin', don't you? And who is this man you done brought up in my house, huh? You brought him here to make a fool outta me! I oughta slap the spit outcho mouth, you ugly ho!"

Noah looked over at Ari. Her breathing was shallow. She was trying to hold back tears. She wanted to be strong in the face of this demon. He grabbed her arm and whispered in her ear, "Ari, don't let her words hurt you."

Ari squared her shoulders. "You know what, Momma? I tried. I really tried to love you. But the truth of the matter is you will never know what it is to be loved if you don't know how to love yourself. I'm sorry my father left you after you gave birth to me, but I didn't ask to be here! You will die a bitter, critical, and broken woman if you fail to realize what you need to change about yourself."

201

"I just want to tell you that all those years of abuse, the time you tried to drown me in the toilet, the many times you knocked me unconscious because you hated yourself, you know what Momma, I forgive you. I really do. You made me who I am. I wouldn't be here today if I didn't endure what you put me through as a child. I forgive you, Momma." Ari's voice never once cracked, though her face was soaked with tears.

Her mom dug the butt of the cigarette into the ashtray beside her. She picked up the remote and turned on the television before returning it to its place on her lap. She then clapped her hands as if a great performance had ended. *This witch is taunting me and trying to make me feel stupid for pouring my heart out. How dare she?*

"You really think you somethin', don't you? You think I care if you forgive me or not? Well I don't. You ain't nothin' of mines. You all yo daddy's work. You ain't never been nothin' of mines! You a Hughes not a Austin you a—"

Ari lunged at her mom, and if Noah hadn't caught her, she would have clawed her face to bloody shreds. The hellish pain she'd buried rose up from her belly and all she wanted to do was kill this woman so she could feel what she felt! *How could one human being be so evil and heartless? Why won't he just let me end her?* Noah grabbed Ari's arms and restrained her as she screamed with tears flowing from her eyes. "I came from you! From *your* womb! I came from *your womb*!"

Ari continued to scream and wriggle as Noah carried her out of the house. Her mother shouted all kinds of curse words as he hurried to get Ari into the passenger side of her car.

He took the driver's seat—Ari was too distraught to drive. The ride was mute except for Ari's soft sobs. Sorrow rode with them.

After backing into a parking spot near Ari's home, Noah got out of the car, walked to her door, and opened it. He kneeled down and held her hands.

"Ari, listen to me. I know it hurts that your mom didn't accept your attempt to reconnect with her, but please don't let it bring you down. I am so proud of you and what you've accomplished. You are a strong, beautiful woman of God."

"I don't know too many people who would have had the courage to do what you did. You found God and you're working hard to live the way He wants you to live. I bet He's very proud of you. You could have thrown in the towel a long time ago, but you pressed forward. Look at you now. I know your mom had no idea about who was standing in front of her, because she would have never acted that way if she did. She will know sooner or later though. In the meantime, all you can do is love her from a distance and continue on with your life. That's the process of forgiveness."

His words were comforting but those familiar stings of rejection vied for her emotions. She just wanted to finally be accepted by her mother. She couldn't stop crying. He wiped away her tears and kissed her hands. "I'll stay with you for as long as you need."

QUEEN ARI
"I used to be a liar, a low down dirty shame..."

Thanks to Noah, Ari's spirits were lifted. He took her to Navy Pier, and they spent the bulk of their day exploring all that it had to offer. They rode the Ferris wheel, enjoyed an hour and a half speedboat tour along the Chicago River, and took pictures at Crystal Garden amongst the full size palm trees, dancing 'leap frog fountains', and exotic flowers. After winding down at Landshark Beer Garden, located about one mile out into Lake Michigan in a tree filled alcove, Ari felt the tornado of emotions subside considerably.

"Noah, I just want to thank you again for everything," she said to him as they walked to her apartment.

"I didn't mind it at all. I enjoy being around you. I hope I was able to make you feel better."

Ari was truly appreciative of Noah. He was so patient, sweet, and kind. *If this were a scene in a movie, it would be the perfect moment for a kiss.* An angelic smile rested on her face.

"You did make me feel better. My hero," she cooed, digging into her purse. Her keys jingled as she pulled them out and turned to unlock the door. Suddenly, a previous conversation she had with Noah crossed her mind. He told her about an incident he'd had at a church he'd visited on the southside of Chicago when he first moved into the city. It rubbed him in the wrong way, and she wanted him to visit her church in an effort to change his perception. She stopped and asked, "Hey, would you like to come to church with me tomorrow? I know you're a little turned off by that other church you were telling me about but—

Noah didn't even wait for her to finish. "Ari, I would love to go to church with you. As a matter of fact, I'm long overdue for a word. I need a church home. Despite the fact that everything seems to be going smoothly, I still feel like I'm missing something. What time would you like for me to come pick you up? We can go together."

Ari's spirit leaped with happiness. "Is eight-thirty too early for you?"

"No, I'll be here."

***

Later on that night, Ari prayed for Noah's healing. He needed to be reintroduced to his first love- God. *I know he can get past this. It's just a fight of faith. All he has to do is trust in God and give Him another chance.* She thanked God for giving her the courage and motivation to face a Goliath that'd basically been taunting her for as long as she could remember. Though the outcome didn't deliver itself to her as she expected, the relief that came with it made the entire experience worthwhile. Something about the future just seemed more inviting than before. However, the tumultuous reunion proved to be unsuccessful in regards to gaining information about her father. She felt naïve for believing her mother would be a reliable source. She resolved to solicit help from THE SOURCE instead.

"God, I want to meet my father. I trust you will help me with this. Amen."

***

"Good morning, Love," Ari greeted.

"Good morning," Noah replied, reaching out for her hand. As they walked toward the car, her free hand held onto the yellow sundress she wore as the white oleander in her curly hair blew in the wind.

His Holy Greatness Missionary Baptist Church was a few blocks away from Ari's art gallery in Bronzeville. The building was a combination of Greek Revival and Neoclassical style, with decorative pillars, heavy cornice, and narrow stain glass windows that reflected a passion for antiquity. Purple tulips lined the outside. Ari could tell the realtor in Noah appreciated the architecture and design of her church.

She took his hand and led him inside. The walls of the hallway were covered with some of Ari's art. It depicted various stories from the Bible. They were greeted with warm smiles, hellos, and good mornings as they headed to a room for adult Sunday school.

After an engaging lesson, they moved to the sanctuary for morning service. The praise team and choir sang, joyfully setting the atmosphere. Any anxiety that would have tried to invade her psyche was denied access during worship. She decided to make a quick run to the bathroom before service began, but she was distracted by the words her pastor used to greet a man that was standing near the door to the restrooms,

"Good morning Pastor Hughes! Man of God, it's good to see you. Are you ready to deliver the word to my flock?"

Ari's heart thumped. She ran into the bathroom and peeked out from behind the door. She saw a well-dressed, middle-aged man with salt and pepper hair smiling at her pastor.

The two men shook hands and gave each other a brotherly hug. Her breathing turned jagged. *So, we just so happen to have the same last name.* It means nothing, she rationalized. She calmed herself down. After relieving herself, she returned to her seat beside Noah in the sanctuary.

Ari felt creepy. She couldn't stop staring at the man she now knew to be Pastor Hughes. Her Pastor was yet to introduce him to the congregation. *Who is he? Where did he come from? Why is he here?*

When the visitor walked up to the podium, Ari whispered to Noah that his name was Pastor Hughes. She wondered if he would catch on that this man had her last name but he didn't.

"A new day has dawned and we should rejoice. Let's rejoice and praise God," the pastor said.

The packed church shouted "hallelujah", "amen", and "thank you". Noah closed his eyes as the chorus of praises continued. "Thank you, God," he whispered. Ari, on the other hand, was being tormented by her own curiosity. *Why is everybody embracing him as if they know this man?* Then she thought about it. *I actually haven't been here for about two months. This Pastor Hughes fella must have slithered his way in during that time and seduced my church family into welcoming and accepting him.* She was seething. Ari didn't care that she didn't know him from Adam. In her mind, the fact that he could possibly be her father validated her prejudice.

Pastor Hughes said, "Go with me to 2 Corinthians 5:17." Pages ruffled around the room as the congregants flipped to the passage in their Bibles. He read,

"Therefore if any man be in Christ, he is a new creature: old things are passed away; behold, all things are become new. Today's sermon will be titled My Name is New New. You may have a seat but before you do, look at your neighbor and say, 'Hey what's up? My name is New New."

The sanctuary carried the echoes of the congregants introducing themselves as "New New" to their neighbors. Noah and Ari said it to each other and Ari laughed aloud, trying to hide her agitation.

Pastor Hughes motioned for the chatter to die down, and then began his sermon. "I really liked this scripture when I first ran into it. You know why? Because after I gave my life to the Lord, I ran into a lot of people who tried to convince me I was the same Ezekiel they'd known prior to me being saved: the same Ezekiel that didn't mind fighting a dude three times my size and the same Ezekiel that didn't mind lying with another man's wife.

You know, they tried to say I was the same belligerent drunkard that they used to party with every night. And no matter how I tried to argue that I indeed had changed, they shot me down all the more with stories of how I used to be." He plucked a handkerchief from his shirt pocket and ran it across his face.

"This happened so much that I myself began to think like, 'hey maybe I am the same. Maybe I haven't changed at all.' But then I ran into 2 Corinthians 5:17 and something hit me. I made that scripture personal and put my name in it. Therefore if Ezekiel Hughes be in Christ, Ezekiel Hughes is a new creature; old things have passed away, behold, old things have become new.

That right there made me happy. It also made me realize I had nothing to prove to man, but there was much to be proven to God. So I stopped worrying about what men thought about me and instead became more focused on what God thought of me, because the scripture said that if I am in Christ I am new.

All those things I did in the past are gone. Now I'm fresh and clean because I am in Christ. I don't know about y'all but I'm glad that all I have to do is be in Christ to be New New." He came from behind the podium.

"Amazing grace, how sweet the sound that saved a wretch like me! I used to be a cheater, but because I am in Christ I am New New. I used to be a fornicator, but because I am in Christ I am New New. I used to be a liar, a low down dirty shame, but since I am in Christ I am New New. Never mind who you thought I was, I am in Christ and I am New New," Pastor Hughes shouted. The congregation responded with claps and amens, sounding as lively as fans at a ball game.

Ari's heart felt like someone tossed lighter fluid on it and set it ablaze. It burned with so many questions. *How could he talk about being new, when the old him left a daughter to suffer hell alone?*

The old him had a daughter he barely knew and the new him seemed not to even care. He's a fraud! She nodded her head, not wanting Noah to see that Pastor Hughes' sermon was making her uncomfortable.

"If you feel uneasy, that's good; it's just the Holy Spirit convicting your heart. But know this—if you are in Christ, you are a new creature, my friend. If you're not in Christ, you can tell God right now that you want to be in Him, and He will make you over. He does not mind you asking Him to make you over. Did you forget that He died for you?"

The choir sang "Make Me Over" by Tonex, and then brought their voices down low. Pastor Hughes spoke over their harmonic humming.

"Don't be afraid to ask God to make you over. He'll wash you clean and forgive you for everything you've done. You may have walked in here unsure of who you are in God. I don't know where you've come from and I don't know what you've been struggling or fighting with, but it is never too late to ask God to transform you.

Do not let the devil make you feel defeated or condemned because of what you've done or who you used to be. You may be acting out because you've been hurt, lost a loved one, been rejected, feel alone, but the scripture says that in all these things we are more than conquerors through him who loved us."

The words rejection and alone singed her soul. Pastor Hughes' sermon may have been vivid, personal, and dead on, but Ari wasn't accepting any of it.

The choir repeated the lyrics, "Make me over again." Ari watched as Noah lifted his head, closed his eyes, and covered his face with his hands. He wept with no regard for who was watching. She immediately felt guilty. He obviously received the word. Tears forced themselves out of her ducts that were previously blocked by indifference.

Pastor Hughes spoke softly through the microphone. "I know you're tired of fighting, my friend. Let it go and come to God."

Noah left his seat and walked down the aisle towards Pastor Hughes, who stood with open arms. The sanctuary shouted "Hallelujah." Noah clenched his teeth and stared at the stain glass windows. "I want to be made over."

Pastor Hughes pulled Noah in for a hug. "Welcome to the family of God," he said. He stepped back and assessed Noah. "God has His hand on your life, young man, and He has a work for you to do."

An usher showed Noah back to his seat. Ari's face was filled with joy as she rose along with the rest of the congregation for the benediction. She was glad for Noah, but if deliverance is the children's bread as the Bible says, God must have forgotten to give her a slice.

Once service was over, Noah and Ari stopped in the lobby area. She had a friend she wanted him to meet. They stood there for about five minutes before they heard Ari's name being called.

Ari turned around and ran to Mischa. They hugged each other like it'd been years since their last encounter. Minus a few texts, Mischa went MIA after the night that she stayed with Ari. Nevertheless, Ari was excited to see she made it to service.

Ari sat her hand on Mischa's shoulder and whispered, "Hey Mischa, who is that Pastor Hughes guy?"

"Oh, he's the new Assistant Pastor. He came from Pillars of the Earth Church in Indiana. He joined us probably a little over a month ago. Pastor made the announcement. But I forgot you wasn't here. And Pastor Hughes wasn't here when you came back last week because he was preaching in Little Rock. Dang, but I thought I told you?"

"No. No you didn't," Ari said a little disgruntled. She was annoyed by this new news. But she didn't want to ruin the lighthearted mood.

"Mischa, this is my friend Noah. Noah, meet Mischa Langston," she introduced.

"Hello." Noah smiled and shook her hand. Mischa's broad and bright smile was pleasantly planted on her face.

"It's so nice to finally meet you, Noah. Ari spoke highly of you. Hey Ari, you all should come over for dinner. I'm making lasagna. You know that's my husband's favorite."

"Where is Prentice anyway?" Ari asked.

"Oh you know, since he finished police academy his schedule is sort of crazy. He had to work the night shift yesterday. He should be home now though. So, did you want to come by for dinner, Noah?" Mischa asked.

He glanced at Ari and when she nodded her agreement, he said, "I don't mind at all."

Mischa lived in Evanston, a north suburb about a forty-five minute drive from Chicago. Noah trailed behind Mischa's car. During the ride, Ari talked about how she and Mischa met in college and how much Mischa helped her when she experienced bouts of extreme depression.

Pulling back the veils from her past now came with less of a struggle because she knew Noah could relate to her. She kept the domestic abuse between Mischa and Prentice to herself though. Turning into a cul-de-sac, Ari pointed to the huge house that belonged to Mischa and her husband. Mischa parked in the driveway and Noah pulled in behind her.

As the three of them walked up to the door of the house, Mischa's husband opened it abruptly. He stood in the doorway wearing his police uniform, the partially unbuttoned shirt revealed a white t-shirt underneath. He frowned at Mischa. "Why didn't you tell me we were having company?" Prentice barked.

She quickly replied, "Oh, I'm sorry Prentice. It was a spur of the moment thing; I just forgot to call and tell you." There was an unmistakable trace of fear in her voice.

The unfriendly vibes spewed from the pores of this dark skinned man, whose long dreadlocks gave him an uncanny resemblance to the movie character known as The Predator. Prentice had to be about six-seven or six-eight in height.

Mischa brushed past him and grabbed one of his hands. "Prentice, meet Ari's friend Noah. He's from Atlanta."

"What up?" Prentice said with his hand out.

Noah gave a cool nod of his head and shook Prentice's hand. The high tension and male ego was real. Ari said a silent prayer because she knew Prentice was an instigator and according to Noah's stories of past interactions with men, he wasn't the one to take disrespect lightly. *Jesus, be a fence around these men. Please!*

The aroma of Mischa's four-cheese lasagna beckoned Ari's appetite. Mischa had already prepared the dish the night before and instructed Prentice to put it in the oven a half hour before service usually ended, at 1:30, so that it would be piping hot when she got home.

"Everyone make your selves comfy," Mischa pointed to the dining area on her left, "while I get dinner on the table." Less than five minutes later, they were seated and had prayed over the food. The first bite of lasagna had hot cheese that seemed to dissolve in their mouths; it was like heaven to Ari. Mischa always slammed in the kitchen. They conversed about various topics over the meal.

"I thought *The Secret Life of Bees* deserved an Oscar if you ask me," Mischa said as she fork scraped the last bit of lasagna off her plate. Ari nodded in agreement.

Noah shrugged his shoulders, "It wasn't *The Color Purple.*"

Mischa laughed, "Yeah you're right. But nothing will ever—"

"Go get me a beer," Prentice commanded Mischa, his rude request sounding as ugly as a piano's discordant note struck in a quiet Opera house.

Ari and Noah looked over at Mischa who robotically rose from her seat, left the room, and came back with Prentice's beer. He stood, stretched, and snatched the beer out of her hand without giving so much as a thank you. Once the bottle was opened, Prentice left the table and walked into the entertainment room.

"Are you all done with your plates?" Mischa stammered. She was obviously frightened and embarrassed. "I can prepare you all some lasagna to take home," she added.

Noah didn't hide his annoyance. "What's his problem?"

"He's a jerk," Ari responded. She got up from her seat and helped Mischa clean off the table.

Mischa attempted to explain. "He's just tired that's all. He gets like that when he's tired."

"Mischa," Ari said, "I really don't know why you accept this man's disrespectful behavior. He needs to be—"

"Ari, please don't." Mischa's shoulders slumped in defeat. She paused from clearing the table and looked over at Ari with a pleading expression.

"Noah, I'm going to help Mischa clean up before we leave if you don't mind," Ari stated.

"No, I don't," Noah responded.

"Did you want a beer as well, Noah?" Mischa offered.

"No, no thank you, Mischa," he replied.

He walked into the entertainment room where Prentice was playing Gears of War 2 on an Xbox system that was connected to a huge wall-mounted flat screen television.

Ari helped Mischa tidy up but stole this opportunity to question her friend since she hadn't spoken to her in person in a while.

The ladies walked into the kitchen side by side. They took turns putting dishes into the dishwasher, and Ari spoke as quietly as she could,

"Has he hit you since the last time I've seen you?'

Mischa ignored her question. She was known for shutting down when confronted with a cramped topic.

"I can't sit by and watch my friend be beat to the ground. Don't you know you're precious to God? You can't tell you're a queen?"

"You're not being treated royally. You don't see that? Why subject yourself to this abuse? You must want him to drag you to your grave? Is that what you want Mischa?" Ari asked emphatically.

Mischa ignored her by purposely directing her focus on cleaning. Ari was irritated. She snatched the cup Mischa was holding out of her hand and slammed it on the granite countertop. Mischa looked down at Ari with eyes drowning in tears.

"What do you know, Ari? You're a public success and a private failure. You're not perfect. Your personal life is filled with smoke and ashes. You don't even know who your father is and your mother hates you. You can't tell me anything. And oh, so you met a guy and you brought him to church. So what! Did you tell him you used to mess with a married man? And did you tell him you had a nervous breakdown and hadn't been to church in months! You can't speak into anyone's life until you've mastered your own."

Did this girl just spit my personal struggles back at me? How dare she? All I was trying to do was get her to see her way out of her hell. Instead, she takes it upon herself to push me dead into my own pool of fire and brimstone. The same pool that I am fighting ferociously to flee! Some friend.

She squinted to fight back her own tears to no avail. Her cell phone in the dining room saved Mischa from a spicy retort. Maybe God saved Mischa tonight from her wrath because Ari surely wanted to dish it to her.

She walked quickly into the dining room to retrieve her phone.

"Hello," she answered tensely.

"Ari! Please come to the gallery! Somebody came in…"

216

The caller was frantic. *Oh, God! Not my gallery!* Ari's hands were shaking as she listened to the rest of the call. It was Evey. Ari's nerves were shot. One mention of her art gallery sent her emotions to a place where she had no control of them. She didn't want to hear anything else. It was time to go.

"Noah!" Ari screamed.

Noah walked out of the room where he and Prentice were to meet Ari who was now in the hallway.

Ari ran up to him. "We have to go to my gallery right now!"

Mischa briskly walked down the hallway with a worried face.

"What's going on, Ari?" Noah asked, grasping her shoulders and bending down to look at her eye-to-eye.

"Please take me to my gallery."

The two of them said goodbye to Mischa and dashed out to the car. They drove in silence, Ari sitting ramrod straight in her seat and letting out shallow, ragged breaths. She wanted to explain to Noah what was going on, but she honestly didn't know herself.

He swerved through traffic like a maniac. It didn't matter how quickly he drove though. Coming from the north suburbs all the way to the southside of Chicago took almost an hour.

Ari remained tense and silent the entire time. Once they'd arrived, she could see the police were there. Fear placed her heart into a chokehold.

As they pulled up, Noah had to reach over to keep Ari from jumping out of the car while it was moving. He parked and the two of them exited the car.

The building had been badly vandalized. Ari ran up to the front of her gallery.

"Ma'am, are you the owner?" A male officer asked.

"Yes, yes I'm the owner," Ari replied through tears.

"Nothing appears to have been stolen but a lot of art was damaged."

"Ari!" Evey screamed running towards them.

"I'm so sorry. I had locked the place up and gone to the café a block away, then came back to this," she waved her hand toward the gallery, "this mess."

Ari seemed to be in a trance as she walked inside the gallery. The huge window had been shattered completely, African sculptures were thrown on the floor, and paintings were spray-painted with red scribble.

"My art. Who would do this?" She whimpered.

She then ran further inside the gallery, completely disregarding the broken pieces of art and glass on the floor. She made a mad dash upstairs to the storage room. Noah and Evey followed. A blood-curdling scream exploded from her lungs. Noah and Evey sprinted up to the storage room. Ari was kneeling in front of her latest painting, "Swinging on a Promise." It had been unveiled and the word ugly was painted across it in big red letters. She was distraught. She felt like that teenaged girl in high school again after discovering her artwork had been ruined. Her world was crashing down before her. Maybe Mischa was right. Her life was nothing but smoke and ashes.

"Oh my God, it's completely destroyed," Evey whispered.

"This is my life! This is my *life*," Ari managed to say. She cried like a baby as Noah pressed her against his chest.

Two officers came up to the storage room to complete the police report. Evey gave them as much information as she could, but she had no clue what to tell them when they asked who she thought would do something like this. One officer placed his pad and pen in his breast pocket while the other handed Evey a card and told her to call the station if she could think of anything else that might help them solve the case. They went downstairs when another officer called for them.

Noah picked Ari up and carried her downstairs to his car. Evey followed, giving Ari a kiss on the cheek and telling her she'd call her tomorrow.

"I don't want to go home," Ari murmured to Noah when Evey went back inside the gallery.

"Where do you want to go?" He asked.

"I don't want to go home," she mustered enough strength to repeat.

Noah decided to take her to his house until she felt comfortable going home. He parked his car and got out. He then opened the door, unbuckled Ari's seatbelt, and picked her up like an infant. Once making his way to the door of his apartment, he noticed that it wasn't completely closed.

Markings along the frame showed that it had been forced open. He frowned, hesitant to go inside. He silently placed Ari down, wrapping his arm around her waist and guiding her to stand behind him. He looked at her and placed his index finger up to his mouth. She nodded her understanding.

Slowly opening the door, he motioned for Ari to stay put outside the door. "I'll be right back," he promised as he cautiously advanced into the apartment.

Ari stood there emotionally numb. She looked over at a butterfly bush and saw something that enraged her.

QUEEN ARI
"The little girl in her began to plead..."

It can't be. Is that really what I think it is? Directly next to the butterfly bush that she'd begun to admire was a spray paint can without its lid. Ari was seething at the idea that was slowly crawling inside the crevices of her mind. She kicked over the can to read the label, *Krylon, Gloss, Cherry Red.* Ari reached in her purse to retrieve her cell phone and quickly dialed 911.

"911 operator speaking, what is your emergency?' The female operator asked.

"Someone's about to die," Ari was able to say through clenched teeth.

She gave the operator the address to a place where she was prepared to kill someone out of nothing but pure rage. Ari walked into the home and went straight up the stairs. She heard Noah asking someone to pray with him. Her face turned up with confusion.

POW!

Ari's entire body shook when she heard the sound of a single gunshot coming from the room where she'd just heard Noah's voice. That sound pierced her ears and rippled through her body. Fear lost the battle to her anger and curiosity as she ran into the room to see a woman in a grey jogging suit standing over Noah with a gun. Without any hesitation, she lunged toward the woman to tackle her. The woman flailed violently and the gun flew out of her hands.

The two women fought frantically and ferociously. They tumbled into the hallway as Ari continued to give this woman, who had a little more upper body strength than she, her entire might.

The woman managed to grab a hold of a full chunk of Ari's curly mane and Ari screamed in agony. At that point, Ari realized she could no longer make fun of all the girls she'd seen in the past, who found themselves caught in one of these grips. *Girls always go for the hair first, Ari! Why weren't you ready for this?*

They fell onto a landing on the stairs, which gave the woman in the grey jogging suit a slight advantage since she was now on top of Ari choking her. Of course this wasn't the first time Ari had been choked. Her own mother managed to choke her until she blacked out. Ari's strength waned, and she thought about what it would be like to die at the hands of this lunatic. Suddenly, the woman's face seemed to morph into her mother's, and Ari found the ability to fight again. She didn't die at the hands of her mother, and she wasn't going to die now! Ari reached up to the woman's face and attempted to gouge her eyes out. The woman screamed and Ari flipped her over and slammed her to the ground. She then sat on top of her and began to pummel the woman senseless.

"Stay where you are! Put your hands where we can see them and stay where you are," a male police officer shouted with his gun pointed at her.

Ari obeyed. A stupefied cloud surrounded her as another officer came up the stairs and placed handcuffs around her wrists. The officer led Ari down the stairs. She was intoxicated by a mixture of poisonous thoughts that caused her to drift into a daze. This moment, this very moment seemed like nothing but a terrible dream. Her daze was broken when she thought of Noah,

"She shot him! He's upstairs! She shot him!"

The officer placed Ari in the back of the squad car and closed the door. Ari saw the woman in the grey jogging suit staggering from inside the home. The woman then quickly ran down Noah's driveway and into the distance.

"Hey! Hey! There she is! Go stop her," Ari yelled.

She sat still after that. There was nothing else she could do in the back of a squad car. The paramedics arrived and quickly went upstairs to get Noah. They came down minutes later, and, to Ari's relief, the white sheet wasn't over his face. *He's alive!* Ari cried. She felt helpless. She searched her thoughts to figure out who this woman was and it all came rushing back to her. *The woman at the Signature Room just shot Noah!*

Ari never thought to ask Noah who she was. She was too caught up in her own life to even care. Now she did. If this woman had anything to do with the destruction of her art gallery, she now had a vendetta against her. The two officers got into the vehicle and took her to the nearest police precinct. Ari allowed them to lead her inside. She shook her head. *This is a nightmare. I can't believe this is happening, I actually can't believe any of this happened!* They removed Ari's handcuffs and told her to have a seat in an interrogation room.

The cold room added to Ari's frustration. She tapped her index fingers on the table, which did nothing for her anxiety. The door opened and a man walked in wearing plain clothes. Ari looked at the man sheepishly.

"Officer Anderson?"

"Ari Tamar," he spoke amiably.

The little girl in her began to plead, "I didn't do anything! I promise Officer And-"

"I know, Ari. I know you didn't. You've had a rough life. I do remember. Tell me what brought you here. You know, if you wanted to see me because you missed me, there were other ways to make that happen," he laughed.

Ari smirked at that small dosage of light in her day.

***

Ari explained everything to Officer Anderson. News of Ari's arrest spread quickly throughout the precinct because she was the owner of the art gallery that had just been burglarized and vandalized a few hours ago. Unbeknownst to Ari, Officer Anderson had been keeping tabs on her since her arrest at age thirteen. She was released without being charged and dropped off to the University of Chicago where Noah was taken to urgent care.

Ari was told she needed to have a seat in the waiting area because she was not allowed to see him. The only information she had on him was tied into the scene she observed from the squad car. Evey ran into the waiting area and went straight over to the seat beside Ari. She'd called her on her way to the hospital.

"What happened?"

Ari shook her head. She didn't feel like telling the story over again. If she did she probably would lose her dinner. She was reduced to a blank stare. She was thankful Evey didn't push for any answers.

An Asian American woman called Ari's name. Ari and Evey stood up quickly and approached the woman.

"He's in critical but stable condition. It's actually pretty miraculous considering the fact that he was shot in the chest. The bullet somehow missed his heart and all his vital arteries. He has lost a lot of blood though, so we aren't out of the woods just yet. You can see him now if you'd like."

The sigh of relief that passed through her lips had revitalized her faith. She grabbed Evey's hand and they ran to the elevator. If Ari had wings, she wouldn't have made it to Noah's side any sooner. The heart monitor beeped at a normal pace, but the sight of him lying there unconscious and connected to tubes was a sobering sight.

"I'm so sorry this happened to you, Noah. Please don't lose faith in God. Keep fighting. You have to keep fighting. You're so strong. You've always been a fighter. Keep fighting for me," Ari begged.

Evey stood by. She wiped away tears, "Don't take him from her God. He's all she has."

Ari held her head down. Blood, sweat, and tears had been her diet her entire life. She wanted to taste joy. Disappointment, a well-known acquaintance, rubbed its fingers through her patience.

"Ok," a hoarse Noah said.

Evey gasped. Ari sniffed and looked up. *Thank you, God!*

His eyes slowly opened and locked in on her. Ari took his hand and squeezed it. He squeezed back with surprising strength.

"Nurse," Evey yelled out.

The Asian American nurse and two other nurses rushed into the room to check on Noah's vitals. Ari and Evey stood back and watched them. Ari didn't really know what all they needed to do to make sure he was ok, but she vowed to stay by his side until he was out of that hospital. She needed him to win this battle.

As the two women watched Noah be cared for, Ari's attention was thwarted by the muffled ringing of Noah's cell phone. She walked over to a chair next to a window and retrieved his phone out of his pants pocket, quickly answering it.

"Hello?"

"Hey. Who is this? Can I speak to Noah?' A male voice asked.

Ari was nervous she didn't know what to say, "Um, Noah's…he's…he's in the hospital right now. Who's calling?

"What? The hospital? Is it bad? Can I talk to him? This is his brother-in-law, Isaiah Sinclair."

Ari froze. *Isaiah Sinclair? As in Dr. Isaiah Sinclair, my therapist?* "Dr. Sinclair, this is Ari. I'm here with Noah. I think he's going to be fine. He was shot. But I think he's going to be fine."

"Ari? You know Noah? Never mind. I'm flying to Chicago right away!"

***

Ari awoke after having a dream she was swimming in a river. But when she got out of the water her clothes were completely dry. She remembered seeing herself digging her feet into the soil by the river and heard a male voice speak, "They will be like a tree planted by the water that sends out its roots by the stream. It does not fear when heat comes, its leaves are always green. It has no worries in a year of drought and never fails to bear fruit."

"Jeremiah 17:8," she whispered to herself. The only reason she was familiar with that scripture was because it was engraved in the wall next to her pastor's office.

She'd talked Evey into going home last night but chose to stay over at the hospital. She wanted to keep an eye on Noah's recovery and she also wanted to be present once Dr. Sinclair arrived. *What are the odds? My therapist is related to this man. That has to mean Naomi is Noah's sister. Wow.*

Noah groaned, causing Ari to direct her focus on him. She quickly got up from her seat, body somewhat sore from the weird position she had to sleep in. She watched him blinking as if there were little anvils sitting on his eyelids. She assumed he probably was trying to make sense of his whereabouts.

"Noah, I'm here with you," Ari spoke softly. *I'm glad I stayed.* She couldn't imagine how alone and helpless he would have felt had he awakened and no one was there.

He cleared his throat, prompting Ari to open up a small container of apple juice sitting on the tray next to him. She placed the straw inside the cup and put it up to his lips. He drank the juice until the container was empty.

"Did you want me to ask the nurses for more juice?" She asked him.

He shook his head no.

'Your brother-in-law called. He's flying up here."

"Is my sister coming?"

"I...I don't know. Maybe so. But I'm not certain." She wanted to tell him that she actually knew his brother-in-law and possibly his sister but didn't feel the time was appropriate. After discussing with him about her arrest and her release from the police precinct, Noah went back to sleep. And a few hours later Dr. Sinclair and Naomi walked into the room. Ari had texted him the name and address of the hospital last night.

"Oh, my brother! What happened to him?' Naomi shrieked as she rushed over to Noah.

"Hi Ari. So, were you around when this happened? Can you even tell us what happened?"

Naomi and Isaiah stared at Ari with serious intention. She couldn't for the life of her understand why all of a sudden she felt guilty.

QUEEN ARI
"Where do I fit in those swirls?..."

December

"Ari are you ready?" Noah asked her.

Almost four months had passed since the devil had thrown everything Ari's way, including the kitchen sink, and she spent her 24th birthday cleaning up the mess from the aftermath. However, she couldn't help but to thank God for His impeccable timing and powerful protection.

Ari grabbed Noah's hand as they walked up the stairs to a two-story brownstone townhouse. Noah had made a complete turnaround after having been shot by a scorned lover who'd been captured and incarcerated for attempted murder and criminal vandalism. Ari's insurance covered the cost of damages and Noah invested capital to have a recreational facility added to the gallery. Noah also assisted her in securing grants she could use to hire graduating high school seniors to work for her studio. She was also grateful that Noah was without any reservations, very receptive about the therapy sessions she had with his brother-in-law, Dr. Sinclair. He was even happy about her meeting his sister Naomi prior to the incident that sent him to the hospital. Everything was coming together peacefully and almost effortlessly for the couple. Today would be like a ribbon tied around her life.

Ari pressed the doorbell to the home and shortly after a fair skinned woman with auburn ringlets styled in her hair opened the door. Her gaze was inviting and warm.

She clutched the opal stone surrounded by small pearls that dangled on the silver necklace hanging from her neck.

"Hi, you must be Ari. Come in. Come in," she said.

Ari and Noah walked into the cozy dwelling, carrying scents of apples and cinnamon. Pictures of family lined both walls in the hallways they walked down to reach the room the woman led them to. She showed them to a fancy burgundy loveseat with mahogany legs. Ari ran her fingers over the gold roses sewn into the cushions.

"Please forgive me. I didn't introduce myself. My name is Camille. I'm Ezekiel's wife," she said as she reached over to shake Noah's hand. Ari held her hand out to do the same but the woman pulled her up from her seat and embraced her. It was one of the sweetest, motherly hugs she'd ever received. It was the type of hug she'd longed for and reminded her of taking a spoon of vanilla ice scream in her mouth and eating it with a piece of hot, sweet potato pie. This woman's hug was like a healing balm to her soul. Like grapes pressed for wine, Ari's eyes burst with tears.

"I know baby. I know you're searching for clarity. I know, honey. God will answer you. He will answer you," Camille consoled her.

Camille was Pastor Hughes' wife. A month ago, Ari confronted him about her belief that he was her father only to find herself opening up a rusty can of worms. Pastor Hughes explained to Ari that he did in fact have a brief relationship with her mother. He told Ari that her mother mentioned him being her father shortly after she gave birth. Though they'd spent a short moment apart, he believed her.

Sometime after that, allegations that he wasn't Ari's father quickly spread throughout the church they both belonged to.

Her mother denied the accusations and didn't confess her doubts until Ari was close to five years old, which is right around the time he left. Ari didn't necessarily agree with him leaving the way he did, but she wondered whether he truly had a reason to stay.

Dr. Sinclair suggested they order a paternity test to bring all of this to rest. To ensure accuracy, they went through a process to receive a court ordered DNA test from the local Child Support Office. It took several weeks before the results were mailed to Noah's address, the place Ari opted for them to be sent.

The doorbell rang and the two women released their hold from each other.

"Excuse me," Camille said, wiping tears from her eyes.

Ari returned to her seat when Dr. Sinclair walked in with a large white envelope in his hands, along with his fiancée Naomi. Naomi's soft expression massaged Ari's heart. Her hazel eyes were piercing but sympathetic. She and Naomi had developed a bond that Ari was unaware she needed until this moment arrived. Her support was more than appreciated. Shortly after their arrival, Pastor Hughes walked in. They all sat down.

The room was crowded with anticipation. Ari suddenly felt nauseous.

"Um, where's your bathroom?" She asked, covering her mouth.

"Down the hall, first door on the right," Camille directed with concern.

Ari quickly walked into the bathroom and closed the door. Her stomach lurched as she gagged. Nothing came up but a belch. She sat on the floor and cried. A soft knock on the door fanned away her pity.

"Ari, are you ok," Noah asked on the opposite side of the door.

Why is he even here? How could he love me as the bastard I am? She felt so unworthy of his support and compassion.

She heard the doorknob turn and watched Noah enter the bathroom. He kneeled on the floor beside her.

"If you don't feel up to it today, we can try it again tomorrow. I just want you to know that you're going to be fine either way. Don't make yourself sick, Ari."

"I'm like an orphan, Noah. I don't have any family," Ari said sorrowfully.

"Ari, you do have family! You have so many people that love you. Don't allow disappointment and pain to blind you, or better yet rob you of the love God has sitting in front of your face. He knew you would be here in this situation right now and that's why he surrounded you with so many people to fight with you and to help usher you into a place of pure joy. Ari, you are favored and you are blessed despite your trials and tribulations," Noah said.

Ari sniffed and wiped her nose. Noah helped her onto her feet. She blew her nose and washed her hands. Taking a quick glance at the pitiful woman staring back at her in the mirror, she let out a sigh of exasperation. Noah grabbed Ari and pulled her close to him. He put both hands through her hair and drew her face to his, kissing her forehead.

He whispered in her ear, "Be anxious for nothing, but in every situation with thanksgiving make your requests known to God. If God didn't give us more than we can bear, we wouldn't need Him."

"Be honest with yourself, and tell Him this burden is more than you can bear. Give it back to Him. Cast your cares on Him, Ari, so you can press forward."

Noah looked directly into her eyes. She looked away. She hated being vulnerable around him. He coached her into taking a few deep breaths before they returned to the room where everyone was waiting.

Pastor Kendricks, the pastor of her church, had joined them in her absence, as well as Evey and Mischa. Pastor Kendricks met her at the entrance of the room and gave her a hug.

Dr. Sinclair waited until everyone was settled in their seats before he spoke, "Pastor Hughes, would you mind saying a prayer before we go any further?"

"Sure. Most gracious and Heavenly Father we acknowledge your presence in this hour. We come boldly before your throne, yet humbly at your feet asking you to place your hands on the heart of your beloved princess Ari as you iron out the issues of her heart. You've witnessed the tears she's shed over the course of the journey you set before her. You know the language of her prayers. You've sat in the corner of her room as she paced back and forth in the midnight hour searching for answers. You saw the abuse, both mentally and physically.

You heard the wailing. You felt her tug on your garments. You were there God, resting in every minute, in every hour of her days. Pull her out of her weeping nights and into her joyful mornings.

Plant a smile like a host of children on her face. Pick her up and swing her around. Let her know that she is yours, that you will never leave or forsake her. Restore to her the days of her youth.

And regardless of the results, bless her with the love she longs for and help her to forgive those who were unable to show her that love, in Jesus' mighty name we pray. Amen."

The room was saturated with a unified "amen". Dr. Sinclair looked at Ari to gain her approval with a nod. He opened the envelope. She grabbed Noah's hand and he kissed hers. Never in a million years would she have thought to find herself seated in her own version of the "Maury Show."

Dr. Sinclair rubbed his face. "Wow. Ok. Ari, Pastor Hughes... is *not* your father."

A few gasps from Naomi and Evey were heard, and Ari rested her eyes on the ceiling. She became fascinated by the swirls in the paint. She noticed how one swirl was connected to a few others but they all created a beautiful unique ceiling.

"Where do I fit in those swirls?" She asked herself.

The traffic of her meandering thoughts were directed away from the ceiling to the image she'd become so familiar with, of a man sitting at a piano playing a melodic song. *That's my daddy. Pastor Hughes told me he plays the guitar. So why did I even hope?*

QUEEN ARI
"Well, they are something blue!"

February 2011

The Rose of Sharon Missionary Baptist Church is filled to capacity with a majority of its members. Ari assumed everyone knew one another because there was an air of familiarity in all of the conversations that took place. She wished Evey or Mischa would have been able to fly to Atlanta with her to keep her company. Her hands were now cold and clammy, and she rubbed them together in search of warmth. She looked around the church and realized that it reminded her of her own.

"Are you related to the L'rieux family or the Sinclair family," asked an old woman who was wearing the color that matched the purple tulips surrounding the sanctuary.

Ari gave the woman a half smile and shook her head, "Neither."

"Oh, I was just wondering cause I ain't never seen you 'round here before. I'm sho glad it ain't rain today," the old lady said.

Ari was glad too. When she left Chicago it was raining and cold, but once she got here the sun was shining and was considerably less chilly. The thought of the decent weather soothed her nerves. She breathed in and out a few times, anxiously surveying the sanctuary.

"Chile, why you so squeamish? It's just a wedding. When I got married to my late husband, Mr. Lewis Dampier, I was real nervous. Sho was. But I don't think my friends and 'em was nervous."

"You calm them nerves, chile," the old lady chuckled. Ari laughed and the lady joined in with her and patted her on the knee, "That a girl."

She saw Noah peek out into the sanctuary and then disappeared. Then a middle-aged woman with a fancy hat came from the same doorway on the front right end of the church. Ari watched as the woman made her way directly to her. She was puzzled as to why.

"Excuse me, is your name Ari?" The woman asked.

"Yes. Is everything ok?"

"Would you come with me please?"

Without hesitation, Ari picked up her purse, got up from her seat and followed the woman down a hallway. They turned a corner and went up a flight of stairs that led to the second floor of the church where various rooms were. The woman's kitten heels clapped in tandem with Ari's new pair of shoes she bought during her visit here in April. She heard low murmuring coming from a room located at the end of the hallway which she guessed correctly was where they were headed when the woman opened the door for her to go inside.

Six women surrounded Naomi with their hands clasped. One of the women was praying fervently for Naomi as all the women held their heads down. The woman who came to get Ari motioned for her to join the circle as she did the same. While they prayed Ari could feel the presence of God fill the room. She no longer felt like she was in a room but on a mountain. Each woman prayed over Naomi and Isaiah and for the protection of their covenant. Ari felt her hand being squeezed by a woman who was holding her left hand giving her the cue to participate in the intercession.

Ari cleared her throat then prayed, "Our Father, who art in heaven. Hallowed it be thy name. Thy kingdom come, thy will be done on earth as it is in heaven. We thank you so much God for showering your daughter Naomi with your love and kindness. We thank you for showing yourself mighty in her and Isaiah's circumstances. And we thank you for the power that you will continually express within this union once they exchange vows and begin to walk together as one. God we ask that you, keep Naomi wrapped in the grace that she needs to be the suitable helpmeet for her husband. We ask that you keep your mercy on reserve for those moments she may fall short of her assignment as a wife to one of your kings. Give her the strength and wisdom to submit to him according to your standards and no one else's. And always remind her that she's a queen no matter what is thrown at her. God keep Naomi's hands clasped to her king's. Let no man pull a part what you've put together. Let your love be made known through this covenant. We honor and adore you God for allowing us the opportunity to witness your true design for love. We bless your name for this holy matrimony. In Jesus' name, Amen."

The room roared with praise immediately after Ari closed up the prayer chain. She was humbled to have been invited to partake in this intimate moment. Naomi gently wiped the corners of her eyes dry and embraced Ari.

"Thank you sister. I love you," Naomi said.

"You're welcome sister," Ari said. Ari wasn't expecting to hear her say that. She held onto Naomi a little tighter. "I love you too."

Once they released from their embrace. Ari made her way back to the sanctuary. But before she left the room, Naomi called her, "Ari, look!"

Naomi pulled up her dress to reveal the same shoes she was wearing. They both were sporting the blue strappy high-heeled sandals with flower prints by Jessica Simpson from Aldo.

Ari hollered in delight, "Well, they are something blue!"

***

The chatter in the sanctuary chimed down when a woman walked up to the elevated section where the podium stood and took her seat near a harp. She played a euphonious tune quieting the lingering chatter. Ari watched as Dr. Sinclair who was dressed in a black tuxedo with a purple tie come from a side entrance with his best man, Noah. She was honored to receive an invitation to witness this beautiful event that she'd heard almost didn't happen. Ari smiled when she saw Noah massage Dr. Sinclair's back and whisper something into his ear, causing him to flash a handsome smile.

Come to find out, Dr. Sinclair had been through his own share of hell and high water as well this summer, which is why she couldn't reach him those few times prior to Noah being shot. By the grace of God, Noah and Dr. Sinclair survived their storms and now had been granted the opportunity to walk into this chapter of their lives together.

The pastor came out into the sanctuary and winked at the groom and his best man. The two respectfully pointed in his direction and returned the gesture.

The harpist changed the tune of her instrument and violinists joined her on stage. They came from the left, front entrance of the church, and took their seats near their violins.

Once everyone had settled in, the musicians played Johann Pachelbel's "Canon in D". Everyone looked towards the entrance to see little girls dressed in purple ballerina dresses dancing while throwing tulip petals down the aisle.

The bridesmaids whom were the women joined in the room to pray for Naomi, came down in their purple satin gowns and perfectly styled coiled buns decorated with rhinestones, along with the groomsmen who wore black tuxedos. The violinists played their violins louder for the arrival of the bride, prompting everyone to stand. Naomi, came down the aisle holding a heart shaped cage with two doves and a picture of their late parents, Mr. and Mrs. L'rieux inside. Ari couldn't hold back her tears. The maid of honor took the cage once she arrived and handed it to the woman with the fancy hat who was sitting on Dr. Sinclair's side. Ari guessed that the woman was his mother.

The music softly dissipated as Dr. Sinclair lifted Naomi's veil. Her face was wet with tears and so was his. "I love you," he whispered. He attempted to wipe her tears from her eyes as they fell. The pastor's expression was placid as he spoke into the microphone,

"We are joyfully gathered here at the Rose of Sharon Missionary Baptist Church to witness and celebrate the joining of these two beautiful people, Dr. Isaiah Solomon Sinclair and Naomi Sarai L'rieux. "Naomi, you may share your vows."

Naomi looked over at the picture of her parents and back at Dr. Sinclair. She dabbed her eyes with her index fingers and inhaled.

"Isaiah Solomon my king, God knew exactly what I needed when he placed you in my life. You were my teddy bear and my blanket when I needed you after my parents died. You're patient and you're so sweet. You accepted me and embraced all of my flaws. The God in you is so strong and seems to grow stronger when I'm weak. You're my best friend and I love you so very much. I promise to love you with every inch of my heart, stay by your side, and fight the devil with you and for you for as long as we live."

The pastor instructed Isaiah to recite his vows.

"Naomi Sarai, my queen, from the very first moment we danced, I knew I'd found a treasure worth far more than rubies. You showed me that you'd be there to fight with me no matter what and I love you deeply for that. Mr. and Mrs. L'rieux raised a very beautiful, strong, Godly, sometimes feisty…,"

Dr. Sinclair laughed. Ari looked around and laughed with everyone else,

"…intelligent, and motivated woman. I promise I will protect you, love you deeply, pray with you, and pray for you as long as we live."

The pastor cleared his throat and spoke, "Will the bride and groom exchange rings please." And they did as such. "Naomi Sarai and Isaiah Solomon as the power vested in me, I now pronounce you, husband and wife. Isaiah you may now kiss your bride."

Dr. Sinclair and Naomi kissed passionately.

Ari clasped her hands together, admiring the couple as they walked down the aisle. Upon talking to them when they came to Chicago after Noah was shot, she found out she and Dr. Sinclair had a lot in common. He was left at a fire station when he was a little boy by his mother and he never knew his father. He and his mother eventually reunited, which is why Ari believed he was so adamant about her finding closure.

Outside the church, Ari searched for Noah through the crowd of excitement and happiness. She hoped he didn't leave without her. She walked through groups of family and friends squinting and silently calling his name. There were children jumping around, taking full advantage of the chance to throw paper confetti at everyone. Ari covered her head as some of it still managed to fall in her hair. She laughed with the children. The joy of the day was unavoidable.

"*Where are you, Love?*" Ari texted Noah.

"Right behind you," Noah said. He embraced her from behind and kissed her neck.

A beam expanded across Ari's face.

"I'm always going to be behind you Ari." He reassured her.

QUEEN ARI
"What did I do to deserve his love?"

August

"Hey Ari, hon, yo' boo is on the phone," Evey shouted up the stairs of the gallery.

"Ok, tell him I'll be down in a second!"

She was painting a new picture titled the "War Cries of Heroes" her depiction of Noah and Isaiah's fight to persevere despite what they'd been through. She couldn't wait till it was complete. She ran downstairs to the phone and answered slightly out of breath, "Hey, Love."

"Hello Gorgeous. How long are you going to be at the gallery today?"

"I'm going to stay here until closing. I want to finish this painting. Plus we're kind of busy. Thank you for promoting my gallery after the remodeling. You're the greatest."

"How many times are you going to thank me Ari? That was so long ago. I told you the people keep coming because God is leading them that way," he giggled. Anyways, I don't want to take you away from your work and all but I was wondering if I could borrow you for just a little bit. I promise it won't be long."

"Noaaaaah!" Ari whined.

"Pleeeeeassse. I need to see you," Noah pleaded.

"Oh, alright. I can't stand you." Ari poked fun.

"And I love you. Meet me by the tree," Noah said, before quickly hanging up.

Ari scrunched her face up, "The tree?"

She shook her head once she realized what he was talking about and became frustrated because of the amount of inconvenience it would create on her part to meet him there. She shook her head. Evey walked up to her. "What's wrong with you, Girl?"

"Noah wants me to meet him by the tree," she said with tension.

"What's wrong with that? That's one of ya'll favorite spots to hang out," Evey told her.

"But I have too much to do and it's busy in here," Ari looked around.

"Girl, I'm here and Mischa's here. Plus the students are coming later. We'll be fine," Evey said.

"Mischa's here? When did she get here," Ari asked.

"Not too long ago," Evey responded.

"Oh I wasn't expecting her to be here. She told me she wasn't feeling well," Ari trailed off.

"Girl whatever. Gone on to the tree. Noah's waiting and you in here playing," Evey insisted.

"But...."

"Bye," Evey said and walked off to assist a customer.

Ari got her belongings and drove to the lake where Noah was. She parked not too far away and walked towards the tree where they often spent to watch the sunset. The wind that blew from the lake was extremely pleasant in the August heat. She squinted to see Noah lying on a blanket under the tree relaxing.

"Noah it's Thursday. Why aren't you at work?"

Noah didn't say a word. He had his earphones in. Ari kneeled down and patted him on the stomach. He opened his eyes and smiled.

Ari laughed loudly, "I really can't stand you."

Noah cackled and sat upright, "You want some pineapples?"

Ari giggled again, "What are you doing?"

"I've had enough. You can have the rest," he smiled.

"You are a mess," she said. She sat down on the blanket to get more comfortable. She shook her head and decided she'd play along with his little game. She ate two delicious pineapple rings and reached for another when she became horrified. She squealed, "Ah! There's a bee in the cup Noah!"

"That's not a bee," he replied.

Ari looked closer although guarded by her extreme fear of bugs, "What is that?"

"That's not a bee," he looked at her cunningly.

She looked at him and shook her head. She reached her hand inside the cup and pulled out the hugest piece of jewelry she'd ever seen. It was an exquisite 14-carat white gold cushion cut one count certified diamond engagement ring. She sucked the pineapple juice off of it and the sun made the rock and its smaller friends dance with sparkles. She cried, "Is this for me?"

"You know you and my sister have an annoying habit of asking the dumbest questions, I promise you. Nope, it's not for you," he kidded.

Ari gushed, "It's just so….so big."

"Well my father told me, the woman whom God would introduce to me would have a very beautiful soul and once I found her, I would have to purchase a ring that matched it. That's the prettiest one I saw in the store. Nothing else caught my eye. Reminded me of you."

Ari gazed at him lovingly and the joy in her morning rolled down her face, "Noah, you are absolutely beyond this world and the kicker is, you don't even know it."

Noah stared back at her with affection and took the ring from her. He looked her in the eyes and brushed her curls from her out of her face, "Ari I found you when my life was really dark and I was unsure about my relationship with God. But everything worked out just the way God wanted it to. I wished you could have met my parents. My father described you and my mother taught me how to treat you." Noah said.

Ari continued to stare at the face of a brave king. *What did I do to deserve his love?*

"Ok, I gotta man up," he laughed and then cleared his throat. He placed the ring on her finger.

"Sweetheart you are everything that I never knew I needed. And you didn't have to do a darn thing to prove it. Ari, the most beautiful woman, I've ever known, will you marry me?"

Ari grabbed her words, "Yes I will, marry you, Noah, the most handsome man I've ever known."

They kissed and then hugged.

Noah took Ari back to the gallery and went to grab lunch for them. She ran inside to share with Evey the news.

"Evey! Evey! Evey!" Ari shouted at the top of her lungs.

"What girl, why are you so loud?" Evey jokingly asked.

Ari lifted up her left hand to reveal to her the engagement ring Noah proposed with.

Evey feigned a dramatic faint and Ari cracked up.

"Oh my Jesus! This is so great! I'm more than happy for you Ari. You deserve it!"

***

Ari was completely engulfed in her latest painting being careful not to make any sloppy brushstrokes. She managed to kick Noah out of the gallery after they all ate lunch. She wanted the painting to be a surprise. Because she was almost done she stayed behind and told Noah to pick her up when the gallery closed. The alarm for the door signaled someone came in. Ari looked down at her watch and wished she'd locked the door a little earlier for the night.

She stopped painting and sat still on her stool to wait and see if the person would leave but she heard nothing. Instead she heard them playing a few notes on the grand piano Noah bought her after the renovation of the gallery. She couldn't play a lick but a lot of clients surprisingly could. She grabbed her Tinkerbell cup full of peach tea and made her way downstairs. Suddenly, the tune the person was playing on the piano brought back a sense of nostalgia; Moonlight Sonata.

As Ari turned the corner, the man sitting at the piano looked up at her. She dropped her cup on the floor and it broke in half.

DISCUSSION QUESTIONS

1.   Childhood trauma, such as physical or mental abuse can have adverse effects on anyone especially if it's at the hands of a family member. Do you think these effects are harder to overcome with or without God? Why or Why not?

2.   Ari had managed to make a way for herself and became a successful business woman. She'd also given her life to God, yet she still struggled with depression and hopelessness. Why do you believe this was the case?

3.   Do you think her ways of handling her issues prior to seeking professional counseling were typical?

4.   What is your opinion on seeking professional counseling? Do you think it's necessary?

5.   If there was someone you knew offering Christian Therapy, similar to that of Dr. Sinclair, would you visit him/her? Why?

6.   In the story, Ari dated, Estavian, her first love, Red, the college athlete, Thaddeus, the older guy, Carter, the married man, then Noah, the pleasant stranger. Did you see any similarities between the men she dated?

7.   Do you believe Ari's choice in men was a direct reflection of the absence of her father?

8.   Ari met Noah during a time some may have deemed inopportune. Considering how the story led, do you believe this was an untimely encounter?

9.   Ari thought Pastor Hughes, the new Assistant Pastor of her church, was her father so she told him what she believed only to find out that he wasn't. Would you have handled this situation similarly?

10. When Ari finally reunited with her mother, she didn't receive the response she was looking for. Were you surprised? What would you have done in this situation? Do you think this will hurt Ari's growth in the future?

11. Throughout the story, Ari had many supernatural encounters with God (dreams) how significant do you believe these encounters were? It was mentioned that her dreaming stopped for a considerable amount of time. Why do you believe so?

12. Ari's friend Evey decided to leave Chicago for some time after the death of her brother Estavian, do you believe this was an appropriate method of healing?

13. Ari's friend Mischa was obviously in an abusive relationship with her husband Prentice and lashed out against Ari when she tried to intervene and give her advice. Can you explain Mischa's reasons for being adamant about remaining in this relationship and what do you think can be done for Mischa to see her way out of it?

14. Other than the main character Ari, who was your favorite character in the story? Why?

15. What was your favorite scene in the story? Why?

16. What is your overall impression of Ari and what kind of life applications did you take from her journey?

IF YOU ENJOYED THIS BOOK THEN YOU WILL WANT TO PURCHASE TANZY ALEXIS' FIRST NOVEL:

<u>TEARS OF KINGS</u>

What do you do when the fight is no longer with the devil but with God? What do you do when everything you thought to be true seems to be turning its back on you?

Follow Noah L'rieux down a journey of bitterness and anger as he blazes through life bordering on the cliff of atheism and lacking empathy for anyone after he loses both his parents. Realizing he has the potential to reap treasures that he didn't even know was in his name, he chooses to seek God all over again. But the fight is real. Will he continue to fight?

Join Isaiah Sinclair as he embarks upon unchartered territory and struggles with his belief that God can deliver on the promises he's made to him. Impatience and lack of trust will cause him to take matters into his own hands. Will he lose the battle and ultimately his kingdom because of this costly mistake?

Discover the significance of another man's life and how he manages to endure heartache, pain, and sacrifice with God's help. See how his life and the decisions he made spill over into Noah and Isaiah's life.

3 KINGS 2 PATHS 1 FIGHT… THE GOOD FIGHT OF FAITH!

BIOGRAPHY

Tanzy was born and raised in Chicago, Illinois. She graduated with her Bachelor's in Finance from Chicago State University. She's a teacher, a dancer, a psalmist, a spoken word artist, an intercessor, and a rising leader in her community. She uses her gifts to minister for various events throughout the city of Chicago. Her goal is to help shift minds and hearts back to God using every gift he's blessed her with. She also plans on writing as many novels as God allows both fiction and nonfiction. So be on the lookout!

www.ingramcontent.com/pod-product-compliance
Lightning Source LLC
Chambersburg PA
CBHW031946240626
47153CB00003B/875